How the Indians Buried Their Dead

Also by Hilary Masters

How the Indians Buried Their Dead

Stories

HILARY MASTERS

Southern Methodist University Press
Dallas

This collection of stories is a work of fiction. Names, characters, places, and incidents are either the product of the author's imagination or are used fictitiously.

Requests for permission to reproduce material from this work should be sent to:
Rights and Permissions
Southern Methodist University Press
PO Box 750415
Dallas, Texas 75275-0415

Jacket and text design by Tom Dawson
Cover photo copyright Joel Meyerowitz, Courtesy Edwynn Houk Gallery, NY

Library of Congress Cataloging-in-Publication Data
Masters, Hilary.
    How the Indians buried their dead : stories / Hilary Masters. — 1st ed.
        p. cm.
    ISBN 978-0-87074-557-7 (alk. paper)
    1. Title.
    PS3563.A82H69 2009
    813'.54—dc22

                                                            2009012162

Printed in the United States of America on acid-free paper
10   9   8   7   6   5   4   3   2   1

For Kathleen

Contents

Acknowledgments

Some of these stories were first published in various literary journals, and the author wants to express thanks for that support and the permission to republish them here. They are the following:

"The Catch" and "At the End of the Hallway"—formerly "Passages" —were published in the *North American Review*; "The Moving Finger" in the *Massachusetts Review*; "Meatloaf" in *New Letters*; "Mourning After" in *West Branch*; "How the Indians Buried Their Dead" in the *Georgia Review*; "Solitaire" in the *Texas Review*; "Shoe Polish" and "The Italian Grammar" in the *Virginia Quarterly Review*; "Where Molly Stayed" in *Nightsun*. "The Italian Grammar" received the Balch Prize for fiction. The author expresses his gratitude and deep appreciation to the editors of those journals for their favor.

Also, thanks to Yaddo.

Meatloaf

His father had asked him about the meatloaf; did he find it moist enough, and could he identify the particular spice in its composition?

"Oregano?" Parker suggested. "It's oregano."

"That's an herb," the older man smiled and corrected him, then wiped the sweat from his face with a clean dishtowel. He winked and pointed a finger at his son. "It's nutmeg. Not many people think of nutmeg and meatloaf together." He shifted in the seat of the booth. "We got three stars on the dish, and no one objects to paying twenty-five bucks for it." His countenance spread apart with amazement, and he pulled the dishcloth around his neck and knotted it to give himself a raffish appearance. Parker could remember photos of his father as he lounged at the bottom of Little Nell in Aspen, a bandana tied around his turtleneck and a glass of something red in one hand.

"That little nut has quite a history. They're from the Moluccas, a.k.a. the Spice Islands. Indonesia. Big wars over them. The English and the Dutch, the Dutch winning out. They had a monopoly for centuries. Everyone wanted the spice—before refrigeration, you know."

"When was this, Dad?"

"Oh, sixteenth, seventeenth century. How's the gravy? You could do with a little more . . ."

"No, I'm fine." But his father had already turned around.

"Hey, Betty," he called to the waitress behind the counter. "Get Jake to put a little of that gravy in a soup bowl, will you?" Then he turned back and leaned over the table between them. "It's a kind of miracle—gravy," he continued. "Just some grease and a little flour, a bit of seasoning, that's all. In the '60s—you won't remember this—but one of those lefty rags sent a reporter down to Alabama during the civil rights business. She was a young girl from a good family, doing her bit for the democratic way of life, and she wrote these stories about how the local folks down there got by. In one story, she said they were so poor that all they had to make gravy out of was grease and flour." The man's face flushed with wonder and his eyes grew wide. "I mean what else is there to make it out of? In her tutti-frutti world they must have used some kind of eau de cologne." His baldness seemed to spill over his brow and into his face to make a uniform nakedness that looked as if it might have absorbed all the heat from the kitchen.

The waitress had set down a bowl of hot gravy next to Parker and paused for a little. He could sense her casual curiosity, looking him over. Was he a new customer or a relative of the boss?—she hadn't yet identified him. He spooned some of the gravy over the mashed potatoes and the slab of meatloaf. It really was delicious.

He had already had a slight meal on the plane, but he could not refuse this food his father cooked. When Parker arrived, his father had emerged from the kitchen, passed quickly around the end of the counter, and pressed him against his sweaty chest as if he were only a boy home from school. His father was all in white—pants, T-shirt, and an apron tied around his waist. He had put on some weight. The diner was empty at this hour, the supper crowd was yet to arrive, and Parker figured there would be a supper crowd. Crisp peaks of linen napkins rose from the tables in the booths, and a range of them followed the countertop that was marked off by about a dozen stools. The traffic on the road outside that led into the city's center was random and light.

Earlier, Parker had looked down from the plane as it prepared to land and as they passed over an enormous cemetery. The exact rows of graves stitched the earth, holding it together maybe, Parker had mused, while next to the cemetery was a good-sized tract development, houses all lined up as if the graves had sewn them into place from the other side of a coverlet.

"Where are you staying?" his father asked.

"The Hilton."

"A fair hostelry. They set a pretty good table. I looked at the exec chef position once, but it wasn't for me."

"You need your own place." Parker looked around the interior of the diner. A tidy bar service glittered near the kitchen door. Betty leaned against the counter next to the cash register. She was looking at something across the street.

"Yeah. That's right," his father replied slowly, tasting every word. "How are the kids?" he asked after a little. "They must be ready for college."

"Jennifer has pretty much broken off communications. I think she's in Mexico. Mark is looking at colleges in Colorado or Idaho."

"Colorado and Idaho."

"The skiing, I suppose." Parker laughed. "Your influence."

"Really," his father said happily. "We had some good times. Once on Ajax I took a wrong turn that put us on a black diamond run, but he stayed with me the whole way. Boy, was he ever mad at me. I never knew a kid that age knew so many cuss words. But he did it—skied the whole run. He must have been around ten."

"Eight—he was eight."

"Only eight," his father repeated.

"He sent his love to you."

"That's nice—very nice. And what of Carol? No love from her I imagine." Parker's father observed a semi passing on the highway.

"After we split, she moved to the coast. Doing well. Some kind of editor for a film company."

"A proper little honey, wasn't she? How I must have embarrassed her—her father-in-law a con. Not what she expected when she caught you, was it?" His laugh was quick.

"That's old stuff, Dad." Parker had been carefully portioning the food on his plate so that the meatloaf, the potatoes, and the pureed carrots would all come out even.

"What do you think of the carrots?" His father leaned toward him.

"Olives, right? You've chopped up olives in them."

"Kalamata olives. Gives you a different attitude toward carrots, doesn't it? I mean, carrots are so commonplace, but there they are—they have to be cooked."

Even in those phone calls from prison, his father's voice had been chipper, the sound of it appearing on the line oddly fresh after the recorded message of the facility that monitored the collect calls. Parker could almost believe the man had just wakened from a nap in some bower caressed by sea breezes rather than in a dreary penitentiary in southern Illinois.

"And your mother of course." The man's voice grew ragged and then halted.

Parker did not look up from his plate. He mixed gravy and potato together, waited for his father to clear his throat a couple of times. "You didn't cause the cancer."

"But I wasn't there, was I? Holy smoke, I have to be guilty of something, or else why am I here? What's the name of that bug guy you write about?"

"Kafka?"

"Yeah, that's the guy. Isn't that his message? You see I did read those books you sent me. Though, frankly, pal, I always preferred something a little more adventurous. Travel books would have been okay."

"There's a little more to Kafka's message."

"Jesus, I hope so. That stuff is pretty goddamn depressing."

What looked like a wedding party rushed by, horns blaring, the lead car trailing streamers taped to its rear.

"Seconds?" His father had gestured toward his empty plate. Parker shook his head and folded up his napkin. He counted the neat triangles of linen napkins rising from the counter. He counted thirteen white peaks, but there were only twelve stools.

Parker had always tried to prepare for those phone calls from the prison by singling out items in the day's news or some family event to have something to talk about, but his father quickly took over the half hour they were allowed to use the phone. His enthusiastic reports of his lawyers' appeals, the complex maneuverings and intricacies of petitions to this or that court made for a far more interesting narrative. And pertinent. For good measure, the man would throw in Dickensian appreciations of the government attorneys and witnesses, some of the guards and other inmates. Parker would lean back from his desk to listen, sometimes fingering the dissertation he had been reviewing when the phone rang. His role as a listener, a member of the audience, was familiar and somehow comforting in its familiarity—his father explaining something, almost a lecture on some arcane corner of knowledge from a phone on the wall in his cellblock's mess hall. The litany yoked them together and passed for intimacy, and he had learned to listen patiently even as his father changed subjects.

"This guy Escoffier was a damn genius, you know," his father had said one evening on the phone. He always called at a prearranged time, usually eight o'clock. "You know about him. French. Born halfway into the nineteenth century and dying somewhere around 1936. Called the King of Chefs. Ran the kitchen at the Ritz in Paris and the Carlton in New York. He invented Peach Melba. You know about Peach Melba?"

"It's a dessert, isn't it?" Parker had asked. "How do you know about this?"

"Interestingly, they have a halfway decent library here, and I ran across a biography. I can also get books from other libraries on a loan system. You name it; I've read them all. Julia Child, James Beard, Marcella Hazan. I've checked them all out. Reading about their cooking almost makes up for the crap they serve us here. Where were we?"

"Peach Melba."

"Right. That shows the man's genius—this Escoffier. Simple ingredients. Direct and no frills. You just take vanilla ice cream and put some peaches on top—fresh or canned. That's another thing: he was big on canning food. Then you add a dollop of raspberry jam and, like they say, voilà—Peach Melba."

"Sounds good," Parker had said. Despite himself, he had been smiling.

"Something extraordinary that never existed before," his father had continued. "That's the ticket. And put together simply. He also invented Tournedos Rossini. To honor the composer, you know *William Tell*— Heigh Ho, Silver, and all that. You sauté some duck liver, sear small steaks, and put everything on toasted white bread. No crusts. Pour brown sauce with port or brandy over everything. Can't beat it."

"Certainly different fare from what you have there."

"But the great similarity Escoffier has with this place," his father had continued without hesitation, "is the organization. Every minute of the day here is organized, delegated. That was Escoffier's real contribution— the organization of a restaurant kitchen. Until him it was a pell-mell, slap-dash affair. Everything cooked at once, and everything served all at once. Courses were his idea—a logical menu where the different parts of the meal could be fitted together. He brought an intelligence to cooking that raised the esteem of the chef, made cooking an honorable profession."

Betty had cleared the table, wiped the marble top, and disappeared into the kitchen with the plates. In there someone whistled a tuneless trill that abruptly stopped. A very large moving van passed carefully on the highway.

"Why are you here?" his father had just asked. His tone was mild, but the casual question took Parker aback because it was a query he had often wanted to ask his father, even ask him now as they sat across from each other in this upscale diner. Why was he here?

"There's a convention in town, and I'm on a panel. 'D. H. Lawrence— Skirting Feminism.' It's supposed to be . . ."

"No, I mean—here," the older man interrupted him. His thick fingers and thumb delicately picked up a tiny crumb from the tabletop and placed it in the palm of his other hand. No doubt, he would hold it there until he passed a wastebasket.

"Well, I wanted to see you," Parker explained. "Neither one of us is great at correspondence. And it's been a long time. Do I need a reason, Dad?"

His father made one of those expressions that could suggest either dismissal or consent. Then he said quietly, "It's just that those of us who go from one life to another, leaving one skill and picking up another, have a tendency to be curious about motivation."

Here it comes, thought Parker, another lecture. But his father said nothing more, and the silence seemed to pull at the son, draw words from him he had not intended to say. "I've met someone I'm interested in. I'd like you to meet her."

"Sounds serious."

"I guess maybe it might be. She's a bit younger than I am—a junior member in the department."

"So you both do the same thing. That's good."

"Sort of—she's in rhetoric."

"That's how to say things?"

"Something like that."

His father nodded. "You've always needed help with that, to be sure. So, you want to introduce her to the old jailbird, the old wheeler-dealer who got caught cooking the books—that's funny, isn't it? Never thought of that phrase until now. At the moment this old guy's slinging hash."

"Clearly, you're not just slinging hash." Parker surveyed the clean elegance of the diner's interior. It resembled photographs he'd seen of the luxurious dining cars on the old deluxe trains—the 20th Century Limited.

"I guess meeting me would be a test of her commitment?" A good-natured skepticism pushed at the man's eyebrows.

"It's quite a story, I think," Parker replied. "Learning to cook in prison and now running a famous place like this." He wanted to say more but only looked around the table, at the art deco salt shaker and pepper mill. Their design was so complete, finished. "At home, I have that picture of all of us on the mantel. We're all together. Then you went to prison, and it was like you had gotten off at some station and we kept going. So abrupt. A kind of death, but you were alive. But we didn't do well on our own. It was like a pin had been pulled, and all our differences fell apart, and we were scattered across a landscape that had, only minutes before, seemed so secure. Together. Like the picture on the mantel. We had only thought we fit together. But I guess we didn't need a lesson."

His father shrugged, and the nonchalance of the gesture, its casual shift, immediately angered Parker. The heat of his anger swiftly rose in his face—he could tell. He hadn't felt this sort of instant rage in a long time. He looked at the man across from him, who was looking out the window, following the passage of traffic with an amused expression. His father looked like a clown, Parker thought, with his bare red face and his dishcloth tied around his neck. The whole costume was a cliché. It was out of one of those television shows, long past its prime time, that continues to run in the early hours of the morning. Even the canned laughter was weary. And what was his father doing but the same old chicanery? The same trickery that had caused them so much misery. Charging outrageous prices for food like this—twenty-five dollars for meatloaf, for God's sake! It was the same kind of swindle that had fooled their family. For a time.

"How about dessert?" his father asked. "Kalimyrna figs poached in red wine. A dab of crème fraîche. It's won a following."

"I'll have to pass," Parker replied. "Susan is reading a paper tonight, and I promised she could practice it on me."

Both men got up from the booth simultaneously and as smoothly as if they had rehearsed and had only been waiting for a cue. Just as they walked to the entrance, a youngish black man entered, his eyes going quickly to the large clock that hung on the back wall.

"Hey, Melvin," the chef greeted him. "Want you to meet my son. He's an authority on Kafka." The two younger men shook hands. "You might want to check the Paulliac," he suggested to his employee. "We have the meatloaf on the menu tonight, and there might be a run on Bordeaux." Then turning to Parker, he said, "Melvin makes the ultimate martini."

"Hey, I learned from a master," the bartender said and laughed. He nodded and turned away and passed through the large swinging door into the kitchen. Father and son stood hesitantly at the entrance.

"It's been good to see you, Dad," Parker said finally. "I'll keep in touch."

His father had taken his hand absently, not really looking at him but at something just behind him, over his shoulder. "I wonder . . . ," he started, then paused. "Well, I wonder if you'd be interested in seeing where I work. The kitchen. My shop."

Parker pulled his hand away. "Sure, why not?" he said and followed his father around the counter and through the swinging door. He had not imagined what the kitchen would look like, but he also wasn't surprised by its orderly appearance and its gleaming rightness.

Stainless steel tables and surfaces lay beneath clusters of pans of different sizes that hung from metal frameworks overhead. A huge stove with many burners and ovens and griddles sat like a massive altar in the center of the room. Several pots of broth simmered on the stove, their aromatic vapors rising into the humid atmosphere. And it was very hot. Parker, ignorant as he was, could recognize the efficiency of the kitchen's design—for example, the relationship of the immense refrigerator to the stove and the workstations was obviously exactly right. An older man was working at one of these workstations, also in the white garb but with a small toque cocked rakishly over one ear. When they were introduced, the sous chef only glanced at Parker and nodded, barely looked up from slicing mushrooms, cutting them into delicate frills. Melvin appeared at the top of a stair into the basement, carrying several bottles of wine in a basket that might have been designed for delivering the old-style bottles of milk. As a boy, Parker had had a summer job doing just that, running up to front porches as the local milkman waited at the curb in the idling truck. In this kitchen, he heard the bottles clink in their basket.

Meanwhile, his father had begun cracking eggs and dribbling their whites into a big copper bowl, separating and keeping the yolks in a ceramic dish. He performed this operation with his right hand, while he made introductions with his other hand, or pointed out particular features of the kitchen's apparatus: the cooker for deep-frying, the warming oven that held two large trays covered in foil. Parker assumed they were the evening's special—meatloaf. His father had selected a wire whisk from a bouquet of implements that rose from a heavy ironstone jar and began to beat the egg whites in the copper bowl vigorously.

"Old illustrations indicate the use of copper as early as the 1770s," his father told him. "But it wasn't until Pellaprat wrote about using copper bowls in the '30s that anyone began seriously to study the phenomenon. We still don't understand what happens, but you don't need to use cream of tartar to make nice stiff peaks. Something in the egg albumen picks up something from the copper. And the result is a creamy meringue with a remarkable resilience. You can't . . ."

"Wait a minute, wait a minute!" Parker had been trying to interrupt and had thrown an arm around his father's shoulder. He attempted to halt the violent whipping of the egg whites that accompanied the discourse, but it was like trying to rein in a runaway horse.

"You want to try it?" His father finally paused and smiled.

"Sure, I'll give it a try," he replied quickly. "Sure."

Parker took the whisk and began to beat the egg whites. His father observed him for several seconds, as if to judge his technique, and then turned his attention to a saucepan on the stove. So Parker must have been doing it right. The colorless liquid swirled and seethed as Parker kept up the rhythm even though his wrist began to ache. He felt a slight resistance develop, and the fluid grew opaque, thickened. It became a heavier lightness. The stiff twirls and ringlets of meringue played like sea foam within the wire basket of the whisk. A sort of miracle was taking place, a transformation that could not be explained.

Where Molly Stayed

She would only tell them that the hotel was in one of those narrow back streets of the Marais near the St. Paul metro and that there was nothing to distinguish it, no sign, only the blue plaque of the Hotel Touriste beside its doorway to indicate that it was a hotel. It had been given two stars.

"Two stars did you say?" Willy asks. "There must be thousands of hotels in Paris with two stars, hundreds in the Marais. We can't go up and down every street checking the bloody markers."

What else did they know? That it had a very small lift, large enough for only two people—only one person with luggage—and a most delicious garden, that was Molly's description—"most delicious," where promptly at four, every afternoon but Sunday, tea was served. The rooms were tidy, with windows looking inward and over the garden, as if to further preserve the anonymity of the lodging's street entrance. And it was cheap.

"Yes, cheap," Constance insists. "I couldn't believe it when she told me the price."

"Cheaper than the Esmeralda?" Willy asks.

"Oh, yes, by far. Forty-five euros with a shower stall in the room."

"Why didn't she tell us where it is? I don't understand that," Willy says and pours some water into his pastis. "It's like a betrayal of the friendship, isn't it? And she was so open about everything else—all those abortions, for instance—and then not to tell us about this find of a hotel. Was that the behavior of a friend?" He's not completely serious.

Randolph snubs out his filter Gauloise and leans over their small table. "She used the place for work. She probably set up that laptop on the high bed. The window beside her and the garden below. Just room enough to stand beside the bed and type, I imagine."

"You're such a romantic, Randolph," Constance teases him. Her perfect teeth make her smile even more winning.

They had agreed that their friend's success was merited; Molly had worked hard. All of them were barely out of Bennington when Molly published her novel to very strong reviews, including that dense essay in the *New York Review of Books* that most people took to be positive. But the second novel had taken years to do, and in fact she had been writing it when she showed up in Paris and pulled them all together again. They had rarely seen each other and had begun to follow different paths when Molly appeared, laptop slung from her thin shoulders, and overnight they were hanging out again—like it or not—just as in the old days.

The reviews of the new book indicated she had avoided the usual pitfalls of the second novel, and they were comparing these reports with almost self-congratulatory excitement when the news came that Molly Stone had been killed in an automobile accident in Southern California. The car in which she was riding had swept off Highway 1 south of Corona del Mar, and the driver had also been killed. Molly had taken the secret of the small hotel with its most delicious garden with her. It really wasn't fair.

Now Constance had called the three of them together to look for this hotel, and their search would be a sort of memorial to Molly, she said. In any event, it would be good to know a place like that for friends passing through Paris. What to do next? They could divide up the Marais into sections all within a reasonable walking distance of the small café where they now sit just across from the St. Paul metro. The place featured tapas. They could also make a list of Molly's other friends in Paris, some of whom she may have slept with, and of course, Randolph had been one of these.

"You swear she never took you there? You never saw this hotel?" Constance demands.

"I swear," he says and sips his red wine. Something Spanish. "She always insisted on random hotels. Spur of the moment sort of thing. The closest we ever came to this neighborhood was a Sunday afternoon after the Pompidou. She had wanted to see the Roland Barthes show. But afterward, we went the other way—toward the river." In fact, Molly had led him down narrow alleyways to a small hotel in a cul de sac where a heavy-lidded Algerian manned the desk. She had gone straight for the corkscrew flight of stairs tucked behind the reception as Randolph paid for the room.

But all that spring the two of them had mostly used his aunt's apartment in the 15th arrondissement that overlooked the Champs du Mars. His aunt had been on the Cap Ferrat with her new husband, a fellow who wore a black patch over his left eye and spoke English as if he were making up the words as he pronounced them. The apartment had a splendid view of the Eiffel Tower, and Molly had flourished herself within its large, open windows that looked down on the park and its contingents of bourgeois families herding their children and dogs below. The clatter of her clogs on the marble floor was among the more pleasant sounds Randolph would remember from that spring, on a par with the fluting of blackbirds at dawn.

Molly had loped about the apartment in that curious loose-limbed gait that gave her nakedness a jaunty flippancy. He could recall the svelte warmth of her against him as the sky grew light and the ruminative gurgles rising from her throat, the small hand that reached to locate him. Every morning she would rise early, and he would discover her standing at the grand piano, where she had placed her laptop. With the clogs on her feet, she wore one of his shirts that fell almost to her knees. Her hair would be piled up high atop her head and fixed with a jade pin that was his aunt's.

"Worked on this new novel, you're saying?" Willy asks. The Rivoli has become busy. "She carried that damn laptop with her everywhere, I guess." He laughs abruptly as if to dismiss the idea.

"She was very serious," Randolph says. He doesn't want to say too much. He watches Constance squeeze her tea bag with its string wound tight around the spoon's bowl.

"We must all agree to that," she says. "No matter what." She looks away, toward a street musician on the corner who is playing an accordion poorly.

"I think she wrote much of the new novel on that piano. The thing should have some sort of historical marker fixed to it," Randolph jokes. He's about to say more but holds back. Willy has never been in that apartment. Nor Constance either, come to think of it. His aunt had returned from the Riviera to sponsor an endless series of soirees for her husband and his business associates. To describe those mornings with the bell jar effect of the light through the immense windows and Molly turning within that light—a figure now gone—might only distance her from them even more.

"But she wasn't all work and no play," Willy observes with a smirk.

"I'm taking the last of these," he says as he picks up a tapas of cheese and anchovies and pops it whole into his mouth.

"She found it hard to relax," Randolph says. Constance pulls her fingers through her hair. He has had no intention of becoming an expert on Molly Stone, but he hears himself continue. "Going to the Louvre, for example, was a workout for her. A rigorous study. I sometimes tried to have fun with the pictures, make jokes, but she would have none of it."

In fact her tense inspection of a painting would leave his humor high and dry; the scholarly horn-rims she wore would slide down her nose as her whole figure leaned into an ancient canvas as if to search for a crack in the pigment someone may have told her to look for. Randolph had endeavored to amuse her with adlib commentaries like the tag lines of cartoons. The several versions of the Annunciation presented a rich field for these witticisms. "Who me?" "Why me?" "It can't be true?" He produced a steady supply of responses to accompany the various expressions of the assorted Marys, and he had been about to apply one of these gags to an *Annunciation* by Simone Martini—the Sienese School appealed to Molly especially—when she abruptly turned around and put her face close to his. What do you see here? her pose had demanded. Please, sir, her stance seemed to insist, won't you give a clever line to the picture of this girl?

In the Marais at the café table, he remembers her face had been attractively bronzed from a longish weekend at Auron. Randolph had seen no point in going with her—only to sit in the uncomfortable lobby of a phony Alpine *hutte* while she mastered the slopes at her breakneck pace. Also, he had made a killing that weekend, trading some used equipment he had located in Zurich to a Brazilian group that wanted to update its Internet service. But her behavior in the Louvre had bewildered him, though the number of freckles that peppered her nose and cheeks had been very appealing.

"I've just remembered something," Constance says. "Molly told me that the *petit dejeuner* in this hotel featured cinnamon buns and gooseberry jam for the croissants."

"Oh, give me a break," Willy groans. "Why don't you let some of those Germans you lead around town look for the place? They could smell it out in no time flat. Gooseberry jam, indeed. You could make it part of the tour—Finding Molly Stone's Hotel." The tempo on the sidewalk around their table has imperceptibly downshifted into the late afternoon lull. No one inside the café seems to worry about them.

"I just know it's near here, probably just down that street." Constance points across the rue Rivoli.

"Why are you so bent on finding this place?" Randolph asks. He could use another wine and looks through the café's glass front for the waiter. "It's a little like going through her underwear."

"A project I'm sure that occupied you more than once," Constance replies. Her toothy good spirits seem fresh, unadulterated. She wears her hair cropped short these days in the current fashion that appears to suggest androgyny but that only seems to suggest the difference in genders was a mistake.

"Super!" Willy claps his hands together. "Where is that bloody waiter? I need a fresh one." He was from South Dakota but had adopted mannerisms of speech some attributed to a British film festival the college had sponsored the spring of their senior year.

"Admittedly, it's on the sentimental side." She speaks to Randolph. "Picking up the pieces. I guess you're right." She places her hand over his. "We can't know everything, nor should we want to know everything."

"Quite," Willy agrees and tugs at his ponytail.

When Molly had come to her door that night, Constance had immediately recognized the look on her face and, without speaking, had taken the laptop from her and pulled her into the apartment. She couldn't remember which breakup had occasioned that look before, more than one probably, and most likely it was that awkward business with the art history professor whose wife, it turned out, had not been as understanding as he had claimed. But this night, Molly's expression was the same mix of defeat and anger, with a faint attempt at the old swagger, and burdened by the pain and the drugs meant to alleviate the pain. The abortion had not gone all that smoothly.

"He wants to marry me," she had said drowsily, as if it explained everything. She let Constance undress her and put her to bed. They slept in each other's arms, a sisterly embrace. They had tried the other once or twice—in school it had been the thing to do—and they had found it all right, interesting but not compelling and rather like reading Colette under the covers with a flashlight, Molly had said.

"Can you imagine marrying Randolph?" Molly asked the next morning at breakfast. She had a good appetite. Constance watched her wind the string around the tea bag and press it into the spoon's bowl. Constance could indeed imagine marrying Randolph, and in the several days she nursed Molly's recovery, making chicken soup, changing the soiled pads and linen, she carefully lifted from her friend's recall as many eccentricities of her now former lover as she dared without seeming nosey. Randolph liked marmalade on his croissants. He could do a fair imitation of Humphrey Bogart and had memorized all the important lines from *The Maltese Falcon*. He didn't like her to use deodorant under her arms—something sweet about that, Molly and Constance both decided. He liked his lamb pink and no starch in his shirts. Oh yes, as for bed, he was athletic, though a bit on the conservative side, but when pressed could be dutiful and rather adroit.

Then why not marry Randolph? Constance had asked. She wanted to fully test her friend's attitude, to be sure the coast was clear. Molly had been intent on a passage on her computer screen as she sat up in bed. Finally she only shrugged. He might be a little dull, Constance had continued. But he wasn't an evil man—meant no harm—and could be a bit droll on some occasions. Moreover, he was clearly on his way to his first million with this peculiar business Willy suspected was some kind of CIA cover. Constance had just put the last of their breakfast dishes into the drying rack when she joked that maybe Molly should have had the baby, and quickly regretted speaking. Molly had jumped up and closed the laptop. She slipped from the bed and began to dress efficiently. She seemed to have checked the clock that ticked within her and discovered she was running late. She put on each item of clothing neatly and in the proper sequence.

"You must understand." Molly had been almost talking to herself. "Some of me may belong to others from time to time, but the ovaries are mine alone. Always."

• • •

"What are you looking at?" Willy asks Constance. He turns to follow the beam of her stare. So does Randolph.

"See that little *librairie* over there? Next to the *boulangerie*? She talked of walking from her hotel to a bookshop to find a thesaurus. It was on the Rivoli, she said, and it had a front window with many panes. Like that one."

Both men look at the store quietly. A few feet from their table, a couple pauses on the top step of the metro to kiss deeply, then descend hand in hand to disappear beneath the ground.

"She said the aroma from the *boulangerie* was irresistible, and she would buy a demi-baguette and chew on it as she returned to the hotel."

"All right—all right," Willy protests. "So, that's the bookstore. So what?"

"You sound angry," Constance says.

"Me? I'm not angry." Willy downs the last of his pastis and checks his watch. He has a shoot on the Isle St. Louis in about an hour, just when the afternoon light hits the old stone facades the right way. His assistant would be there already, setting up the equipment. The dresser would be there as well as the model. He has worked with her before. She is a Polish girl and new in town and something of a cow, he thinks, but has one of those faces that must be photographed before she turns twenty-one.

In Auron, weather had held up the shoot, though the storm had actually created the quality of light for which Willy's pictures were becoming famous. But this time, the editor had asked Willy for hard contrasts between the materials of the clothing and the chiseled inclines of the French Alps. The pictures were for a fall issue.

The fresh powder had also brought hoards of new skiers to the resort, and this new invasion had included Molly lugging her laptop. She had sweet-talked his answering service into telling his whereabouts, and he would just have to put her up because there wasn't a single room available in town. She had to get away from Randolph for a while, take a break, and this last reasoning had swayed him.

Together they went to a ski shop to rent some equipment for her. A young man fitted her into boots and chose the proper skis for her level—she admitted to being an advanced novice—as he turned upon them one of those round, pugnacious countenances to be seen in medieval tapestries and that still regard the doings of the contemporary world with a surly bemusement. He seemed to take both of them in at once.

But the equipment remained stacked in the foyer of Willy's room and was never used. Molly set up her laptop on the small balcony and worked on her novel morning to night. She ordered *petit dejeuner* from room service and left the room only for dinner, which meant that Willy could never use the room during the day. The sun had returned with a stunning force, a white on whiteness that set his light meters humming. He never trusted them anyway, particularly in this brilliance, and he bracketed each shot no matter what his meter registered. He finished the shoot in one day, on a morning of crystal purity, which left him free. Claude, the young fellow in the ski shop, had been more than agreeable, but with Molly pursuing her muse in his hotel room, they had to make do in the back of the shop. It smelled of varnish and warmed wax and was cluttered with ski poles and skis at all angles—all of which lent a raffish quality to their endeavor.

The sun's return had also urged Molly to shed her clothes, and she worked on the balcony outside the bedroom wearing only a pair of his boxers. If any skiers had noticed her—the bottom schuss lay just below the room's windows—their observations would have been fleeting and casual. In spring, some young women even skied topless. But Molly's breasts were exceptional, Willy had judged them. Not overly large, they sat high on her chest, as if modeled by Bernini, their firmness a secret within their supple volumes.

One night, he saw her studying her breasts in the bathroom mirror as they prepared for bed. "What's the matter?" he asked.

She had paused scrubbing her teeth. "Gravity," she finally answered. "Gravity is the matter."

Willy considered doing some nudes of her—just the torso—and she would have had no objection. But to make a permanent record was somehow a transgression; yet he studied her breasts as if he were focusing his Nikon on them. Something vague had affected their exact proportion, a quality that edged their perfection to one side and made just the shadow of a difference. Molly had looked up from the keyboard, as if his scrutiny had alerted her. She nodded and returned to the paragraph she had been shaping.

"You don't mean it?" Willy exploded into laughter. "Pregnant?" She had nodded once again, never slowing the rapid play of her fingers on the keyboard. "You bloody alley cat," he admonished her. Molly had giggled slightly and pulled herself together, crossed her arms as if a sudden chill of modesty had caressed her. Clearly, he had interrupted her morning's work, so she took a shower, dressed, and poked around the village.

She was not the first woman Willy had slept with. In college a valiant young woman had attempted to give him a balanced view of the possibilities, and he had always been grateful, but enough was enough. Nor was he uncomfortable sharing his bed with Molly; his ease was cushioned by her instinctual sense of propriety. She understood there were territorial limits to be observed. Her circumspect manner preparing for bed had surprised him a little, and then she lay demurely on her right side, turned away from him on the edge of the mattress, one hand clasped between her thighs. She wore one of Randolph's T-shirts that came below her knees and completely enveloped her. *Hub-a-Hubba* was printed on its front. Willy would wake in the night to the gentle rain of her laptop keys pattering in the bathroom as light seeped from beneath the closed door.

But his notice of the slight change in her breasts had also made her focus on a possibility she had only glanced at—seeing but not seeing. So he felt responsible for her sudden change of plans; she abruptly decided to return to Paris and announced her decision that night at dinner. They drank too much brandy, and Willy had already been out of sorts. Claude had been silly and coy that afternoon, telling in tiresome detail of a matron from Nice who complained her ski poles were not right for her. She needed something longer. So tiresome, the boy's crude attempt to rouse his jealousy had only reminded Willy that he should play in his own neighborhood. But different streets did sometimes offer a particular excitement.

"Does he really say that?" he asked Molly after their third brandy. "Hub-a-hubba."

"Only in moments of inarticulate delight," she answered. Her laughter was so intense as to be soundless. White lines appeared beside her nose, and she finally let loose with a rowdy gust of amusement. She took a swallow of brandy and became quickly serious. When she squinted, the small features of her face became even smaller. She stabbed the nail of her index finger at him. He must never tell Randolph about this. Never, never, never. Swear? He would have to swear. "Here"—she grabbed up the ashtray on the table and placed it before him. "Swear, never to tell Randolph." Willy put his hand on the ashtray and swore himself to silence. It was an easy oath to take and easily kept. Randolph was just the sort of guy, so well meaning and straightforward, over whom it would be fun to hold such a secret.

That night a cool wetness on his cheek woke him. Molly had leaned over him, and the tears of her soundless weeping fell upon him. She asked him to hold her for a little, and he did. She lay against him with a childlike confidence, a snuffle and a hiccup, and the gentle articulation of her body fitted neatly into the gradual awareness of himself. It was a rare moment. Just before dawn, she cleared her throat. "I thought it would be so easy," she whispered.

"Are you off?" Randolph asks. Willy has stood up.

"I must dash." He puts down some money on the table. "Keep in touch. If you find the hotel let me know. We can meet there for tea some afternoon."

Constance and Randolph watch him until he quickly turns the corner and disappears. Just the two of them now, and a restlessness joins them at the table. The scary notes of an emergency vehicle warn everyone of its approach. Then the siren suddenly stops. Randolph waves at the waiter.

"It was so sultry today," Constance says, fishing in her purse for some bills. "I must be on the odiferous side. I've stopped using deodorant. It gives me a rash." She shares this intimacy with a laugh and leans forward into her blush. Randolph only nods as he carefully reviews the bill. He makes an orderly pile of their monies, leaving an extra amount on the side for a tip. He tells her he is going to Budapest in the morning, but he will be back toward the end of next week. Maybe they could have dinner? Constance says that would be great. Just great.

At the End of the Hallway

He would remember the corridors of that last, best establishment always seemed ready to end, but then, with an unexpected jog or a rise of two steps, another hallway would range deeper into the ramshackle mansion toward one more room, one last closed door. Often, he stopped to listen at some of these doors, and he became acquainted with the roomers behind them by the particular sounds they made, a cough or scrape of footfall, a radio program. Sometimes, he heard peculiar scratching noises as if the occupant within was burrowing deeper into the plaster walls and oak floors of the rooming house his grandfather owned.

His own room was at the very top, above all the narrow hallways and the closed doors, and within a curiously windowed loggia that looked out on three sides and down on the boulevard below. Later, he would wonder if its design had been a whimsical afterthought of the architect grown bored with the commonplace first three floors he had been commissioned to design. In any event, this elevation made for a daring, exclusive perch from which he could look both ways down the avenue before the house. He could monitor the passage of streetcars as he did his lessons, bathe in the reddish gold of sunsets, or, occasionally, at dawn almost feel the large house tilt slightly beneath him to frame the morning sun in the opposite window.

It was like a cozy tree house, his alone, and he had fixed it up with all the serious excitement of a Robinson Crusoe, amazed by his own ingenuity with orange crates and odd hangings, not to mention the possibilities of cornices and cabinetry that carpenters had fashioned to satisfy the architect's offhand inspiration. A dig into these sites would reveal the genealogy of his tenancy: mysterious pieces of yarn, tops, and lead soldiers, a birthday card from a grade school sweetheart, and, finally, a catalog with pictures of young women indifferently standing in their underwear.

Aromas, too, had collected in the hallways to rise in a stale buoyancy to his floor, but they never became offensive. On the contrary, their mildly fecal nuance so saturated his sensual tissue that later in life, he could easily recall their odors by holding his fingers beneath his nose. Scraps of sound also drifted from the black iron grill of the heat register beneath a window seat as if from the speaker of a poorly adjusted radio, a jumble of faint music and a comedy program. Of these, he could always distinguish his grandmother's radio playing in the back room next to the kitchen on the first floor. When they had moved into this final outpost, when the family house had been sold, she had curled into the sheets of her bed to follow the misadventures of Jack Benny or Fibber McGee and Molly. He had learned the comedians' routines, their timing, sometimes pausing in his homework to anticipate the punch line coming through the register, the anticipated sound effect that exploded the laughter of a studio audience.

In their first weeks at this last address, he had gone into her room to sit by her bed and share these programs with her as they crackled from the Bakelite case of the radio at her bedside. Once or twice, a gnarled, withered hand would shyly come forth from beneath the coverlet, and he would obey its silent entreaty and close his own upon its skeletal shape. Hand in hand, they would listen to the domestic farces that stirred so much laughter in the square box of the radio, but his own routines, schoolwork and neighborhood play, eventually drew him away from her bedside, so he could only share the programs through the heat register of his room. Then, one evening, an abrupt silence, as if the radio had been turned off in the middle of a joke, even before its laughter had begun. He always thought the interruption had been unfair. In fact, his grandfather had turned off the radio that Sunday evening and then walked down the street and brought back a doctor who lived several houses away. The end of those broadcasts also signaled another change, as if turning off that radio had given his grandfather the license to start shutting down the rest of their lives. Perhaps those old vaudeville routines had bound them together, and they had become undone in the silence.

By then, of course, he had also given up his dutiful watch of the streetcars that stopped before the house and had become resigned that his mother would never get off one of them. He had imagined how she would do this—stepping down from the car, saving a little hop for the last step to the pavement, her purse pressed close to her bosom. But he would never see her face. From his high prospect, he would only be able to see the top of her head. If there had been pictures of her on the mantel of an earlier house, he could not remember them, and her image had been banished in subsequent domiciles when she had banished all of them.

So, in his mind's eye, he would follow the top of her head as she crossed the boulevard and advanced to the sidewalk before the house to disappear beneath the broad overhang of the front porch roof. In winter, she would wear a dark turban, exotic and of the Orient—he had seen pictures of some in a magazine—but something lighter in spring and summer, a straw hat, perhaps with outrageous cloth daisies at the brim.

In warm weather all the doors and windows of the enormous wreck were wide open, and he would sometimes cock his ears and put down the model plane he had been assembling to attend voices at the front door far below. He might have missed her. She had not come by streetcar but by a yellow cab that had stopped around the corner, and she had come up the sidewalk and across the lawn and up onto the porch. He would strain to hear the exchange at the front door, sounds of surprise, perhaps angry words right off, and then murmurs of reprieve sifting through the big screen door his grandfather was always repairing. But no, only the usual sounds would drift up through the register, the muffled hack of the old soldier on the second floor, a closet door in another part opened and closed discreetly.

His mother had left all of them, not just him, though he had first reasoned that she had gone to look for his father, who had left her as well. It was a funny sort of relay that would occupy him as he fell asleep, following the lights of a late night streetcar moving across the ceiling above his bed. If that chain of events could only be interrupted at one point, they might be all together once again. Sometimes, as he drifted off, he imagined her fierce and strong, like a comic book superwoman, her cape unfurled as she pulled this vagrant man up by his collar and shook some sense into him. Other times, she would appear like one of the young women in a secreted magazine, toothsome and insouciant in their near-nakedness, but this fantasy would make him uneasy, though he knew she wore underwear and must resemble the models in every way.

His sentry duty had long been resigned when one afternoon he swung down off the streetcar, his book satchel a parachute pack that had become tangled in novels with stories about boys abandoned and put up for adoption only to become well off. If he could just land safely, he might evade the panzer division closing in, but he saw his grandfather pounding a FOR SALE sign into the baldpate of the terrace before their house. So that afternoon, he landed on the pavement a little winded and flat. He looked up. Through the softening buds of the elms, he saw the wide, high windows of his crow's nest and through the large glass panes, he made out the corners of pictures he had tacked to the room's walls, the closet door he had left open that morning. The great bulk of the house seemed to shift, disengage, like a ship almost imperceptibly coming off its mooring, about to make way and leave him stranded on this streetcar island in the middle of the boulevard.

"It is time," his grandfather told him. They were fixing their supper in the high, dark kitchen at the back of the house. The door of what had been his grandmother's room was closed. Porch chairs and snow shovels were kept there now. "I can no more do this," the old man said.

Unattended and unapplied, the pronoun could refer to the meat frying in the pan as well as his operation of the rooming house, collecting the rent and making the endless repairs. Or, he would think later, his grandfather had referred to waking up morning after morning in the dim front room on the first floor. Or it could have applied to the two of them, man and boy, their relationship, the pain it caused the old man just to rise from his lounge chair every afternoon to ask about schoolwork, even that schoolwork now far beyond his expertise. The *this* had become a burden too heavy for him to even articulate.

"I have figured it out," his grandfather continued, turning the smoking meat in the pan. He had been a fireman, and the boy often wondered if his method of cooking had some connection with the conflagrations he had battled as a young man, lashing burly, ferocious horses through the night, then, just before his retirement, gripping the enormous steering wheel of a heavy, tired machine.

"You'll have a roof over your head, and you'll get a good education," he had continued. "That's to be kept in mind. Your reports are good, and the state university is a fine institution. I've paid taxes for it." He had put plates on the kitchen table in the middle of the large room. This kitchen with its tall, glass-fronted cabinets on three sides had been planned for a staff of servants. His grandmother's room had been the pantry, so at meal times, the very volume of emptiness seemed to press the two of them into a greater intimacy. As the meat fried, the boy's job was to choose a canned vegetable from the store kept in a cabinet over the sink. Peas, carrots, green beans, spinach, succotash; the selection never mattered to them, for the contents all tasted the same. Potatoes had been boiled in their jackets and waited in their cooling water.

All that spring, his classmates had talked happily of their college plans; their applications to different schools had been accepted. Quietly, he had listened to their excited buzz as he tried to picture himself on a university campus, a wide pastoral vista with the muffled sounds of a football game in the distance. In fact, similar sounds had risen from the heat register as the roomer on the third floor tuned in to the contests. Cornell. Purdue. Northwestern. Notre Dame. The names had seeped into him like the recitations of an oracle, ancient and sacred sites that he knew instinctively were not a part of his destiny.

On the cover of his notebook, a couple leapt high in the air, holding huge megaphones. The girl resembled the young women in the magazine hidden behind the molding, though she was dressed in a flaring skirt and a heavy sweater. The young man wore a similar sweater, and on both a large capital *D* had been fixed. He had spent almost an hour in the school library looking up the names of the colleges this exuberant pair might have cheered to victory. Dartmouth. Dennison. Drake. Davidson. Duke. Duquesne. He had made a list and tacked it to the wall next to the map of the world above his bed.

So, the thought of going to college had occurred to him, but his grandfather's announcement had astonished him. That evening, after they had done the dishes, and after he had climbed up to his room to do his homework, he stared at the cover of his notebook. He put himself into the saddle-shoes of the boy in midair, and he fell in love again with the girl. Her smile alone enabled her to defy gravity. That he could be in that picture, hold up one of those megaphones—the letter *D* was totally inappropriate for the state university—stunned him. It was like finding pieces of gold on the sidewalk in front of the house. He looked around his room to assess his belongings: the small plane models hanging on slender threads from the ceiling, arrangements of marbles and fish bones. All worked a sad alchemy to dissolve his excitement. The boulevard below was washed by automobile lights, and a near empty streetcar trundled by without stopping. He would lose this observation post.

"It's too much for me to handle," the old man had said.

"But what about you? Where will you go?"

"There's a fireman's home in upstate New York. I've paid into it over the years. Comfortable place. Has everything I will need."

How like the old man to arrange their future in this practical manner. He had confronted the decay of the old house in the same way, attending each breakdown with just the right amount of repair at the right time. A long piece of wire in his toolbox waited to bandage a patch around a drain on the third floor when the corrosion finally worked its way through the metal. His grandfather had probably reviewed this plan to send him to the state university for years, turning it over in his head like the pages of an old history book, as his grandson had slept unknowingly, high above.

"You'll be far happier with your own kind," the old man said with a wisdom that concluded the topic, though he might have been addressing himself as well. The boy could imagine his grandfather sitting in a large sunporch at the end of rows of neatly made beds, trading stories of disasters with other old firemen, talking of the power and capacities of different water pumps. Perhaps, in all those years of nursing the recluse in the room off the kitchen, all those complaints that had collared him on stair landings and in the hallways, the problems with hot water, broken linoleums, the screens—always the screens—that needed repair; perhaps, in all those years the old man had hungered and planned for this idyll, this place of reminiscences from more challenging times, genuine emergencies that carried the possibilities of heroism. For a time, they would write to each other, his grandfather's hand becoming more and more spidery as the messages set down cautions on incurring debts, certain foods, and women.

And what about the room off the kitchen? Where would its aromas of lavender sachet and powder go, the dried flowers in the Haviland vase on the bureau? The radio? Several times, he had come into the room to sit on the empty bed and reach over to turn the knob of the radio. The dial's light would surprise him, and the familiar sounds within the plastic box seemed to pick up where they had been turned off—the same comedians telling the same jokes on Sunday evenings. He would watch from his perch for his grandfather to emerge from beneath the porch and walk down to the corner park, where games of checkers were played in the evening. Once the old man had turned the corner, the boy would slip down the stairs to the small room off the kitchen and sit on her bed and listen to the radio, sometimes laughing out loud. How could these silly jokes have penetrated the thick blanket of despair she had pulled over her head? Or had the jokes even interested her? Maybe the audience's laughter had cheered her a little. Or perhaps those anonymous hoots and giggles, a monotonous hilarity, were a response to what her life had become. He promised himself, the day after his grandfather's announcement, he would never leave this radio behind.

"But look," he said to the old man the next night. "I can take care of this place, come back on weekends." They were frying small steaks. "The university isn't that far away. You don't have to worry about the house at that place in New York. I can handle everything for you."

"No, it's done," the old man said.

"Done? It's sold already?"

"No, but it will be. It has to be this way."

"What if I don't go to the university? What if I stay here?"

"Stay where, boy?" His grandfather's tone was more amused than impatient. "Where will you stay? How will you live?"

"I'll get a job," he replied. He felt they were being overheard. His grandfather slowly shook his head and moved the frying slabs of meat around in the pan with a long fork. "Are you sure you can find a buyer?"

Who would buy such a derelict, he had almost added, but the words had lumped in his throat, and his eyes stung with his own disloyalty.

"Someone will buy it," the old man said with a smile. "Here. Pass your plate."

So, like all the repairs his grandfather had made to the old house, he too had been put right—the university was everything he had ever dreamed of and more. The campus was a verdant acropolis, and he joined the roar in the stadium, the endless excitements in the classrooms. The cover of his old notebook had come to life, but he had not brought it with him. He had left it precisely in the center of his desk in his room high above the boulevard.

His grandfather's first letter told of the quick sale to the first comer, more of a transfer of deed than an actual passing of money, the letter written and posted from the railway station as the old man was about to board the train for New York. It was as if he had been afraid the transaction could be called back if reported from any other location. The new owner wasted no time hiring a crew to demolish the house and prepare the lot for a new building. "It is to be only two floors," his grandfather wrote, "a dry cleaners on the first and an insurance office on the second. He'll have to do something about parking. Be a good boy," he added.

Sometimes, if his roommate stayed out late, he would quietly play the radio by his bed. The dim glow of its dial would gradually define everything in this new room, this new arrangement that was becoming his own. He would listen to the music of dance bands on remote broadcasts from around the country, their throbbing rhythms playing against his drowsy pulse as he visualized the old house being taken apart from the top down. Piece by piece, the workmen removed the structure, and sometimes they would pause in their demolition to look over curious items left behind by the former residents: pin cushions and souvenir ashtrays, old letters, magazines, pieces of yarn and pictures of innocence, for the first and last time, revealed.

Chekhov's Gun

A friend gives this account of one of our diplomats and his romantic involvement with a young musician, a member of the Conti Trio. The group had begun to receive worldwide recognition when the two met in Helsinki.

But to call him a diplomat is to foster a false image of the man as being Eastern Establishment and privileged, when in fact, he was from Nebraska, from a farm family, and had worked his way through several degrees in economics and had been teaching at a college of modest distinction when the Foreign Service recruited him.

His name would never appear in news stories, nor did he seem to have a particular post but would show up frequently in the foreign camps of our nation's crusade for freedom, often when a country's leadership changed with a transition not always peaceful. If he ever appeared in a photograph, he would be one of a group standing in the rear of a press conference, unidentified, and with a distracted look on his face, as if looking outside the picture toward his next assignment. In all probability, these commissions carried danger within what looked like ordinary portfolios, and the man's very banality contributed to his success in these precincts. He appeared to be an agreeable salesman of some kind—a trusted uncle—who had blundered into the wrong reception but was invited to stay nevertheless because of his easy geniality. So his intense affair with this vibrant young woman, whose passionate playing of the cello had stirred audiences worldwide, was never suspected.

Sometimes, even Adela Pelus would wonder how this nebbish bureaucrat could fine tune her ardent nature—a man comfortably married and her father's age—who would unexpectedly appear in Berlin or Warsaw or Copenhagen to claim her as the applause petered out and take her plainly on some piece of furniture in her dressing room before she had even put away the Amati. The whole affair was egregious; she could not explain her compulsion, nor did she even like the phenomenon of their relationship, as she had told him more than once in early morning splats of anger that pieced together her frustration with these rendezvous. To say that he was different from the other men in her life was not enough, and she became wary, watchful for these encounters, learning to anticipate them by scouring newspapers for reports of unrest or revolts in parts of the world that might coincide with the trio's concert schedule. Her colleagues, the other two women also attractive and adventurous, teased Pelus on her sudden interest in international relations, but they were unaware of her study's motivation. So the couple's subterfuge was assisted by the very incomprehensibility of its passion. In her colleagues' eyes, the diplomat was only the familiar figure of the older man, an ardent music lover, usually encountered on tour, whose erotic ambitions might be satisfied by the frisson of a kiss on both cheeks. During their boring travels between appearances, the pianist and the violinist would openly talk of their own liaisons, but Adela Pelus would add nothing to their handbag of sensual mementos. They had always regarded her as cold, surrendering only to the demands of her music, into which she put her passionate nature.

All three were stunning women, and there had been some talk that the Conti Trio had been assembled—*packaged* may not be too strong a word—as much for its sexual image as for the musicianship of its members. The picture of Adela Pelus bending over the instrument between her thighs became a metaphor that identified the group, just as her playing contributed to its success.

The scarf of her russet hair fell over her fingers as they pressed the cello's board so the graceful curve of her white neck was exposed, her other arm raised as if to embrace the sounds of the music while her torso swayed to become one with the instrument. The audience was challenged not to look away. That evening in Helsinki, the diplomat discerned a discipline within her fiery abandon that sounded something similar in his own being.

The trio's program that night was made up of South American composers, featuring the music of Ástor Piazzolla, influenced by the tango, as a tribute to the surprising affection the Finns have for this mode. The diplomat had only just been in South America, leaving prior to the assassination of an influential cabinet minister in Brazil. He was to spend a few days in Helsinki, a sort of disappearing act that was part of his protocol, before returning to America and a brief visit with his wife and family. His wife was a good-hearted woman who cheerfully kept house and ignored his frequent absences as she had supplied amiable evenings and baked goodies for his students when he had been a teacher. His assignments were tucked into the complaisant folds of her innocence.

Someone in the embassy had invited him to the concert and the reception later, and it had been a tumultuous evening. The Conti Trio had taken Helsinki by storm. Adela Pelus, tossing her long reddish hair as she rendered Piazzolla's fortissimos, had ignited the audience. The diplomat was also moved. He became aware of a curious prudence within the voluptuous cadenzas, a discretion he could identify with. She practiced a judicious violence—to give it a distinction—that was within his calling, and he determined within the darkened auditorium that he would possess her.

He had constructed a reasonable morality for himself that eliminated dalliances because of their sometime impracticality and distraction. He brought the same judgment to his assignments, and his superiors were pleased. Though the opportunities for such diversions were plentiful and as tempting as the array of canapés spread wantonly during official gatherings, he had never partaken. "Simpson is all business," it was said of him, and the characterization had become part of his file.

But as he listened to the music that night in Helsinki, the chords the young woman pulled from the cello set up a vibration within him he could not deny. How to shape an affair around their peripatetic lives also challenged him and excited him by its very instability, its continual commencements that would eschew the humdrum. The trio began the final part of their program, a piece by Villa-Lobos. The cellist seemed to be limning her very soul with every thrust and pull of her bow, exposing herself completely. The standing ovation demanded an encore—a spirited *au revoir* Simpson could not identify. He had already determined that a shelf in Hell awaited him because of his different endeavors—and for what he had recognized from the beginning as a betrayal of his students' trust—so what matter that his career and constancy, his discipline and tact, might be compromised a bit more? He applauded even louder, his cries rising above those around him like those of a drowning victim.

At the embassy reception, he quietly made his way through the crowd to stand just behind her as she chatted with a young man who turned out to be a German composer who hoped to gain her interest in one of his compositions. Simpson listened, observing only part of her face and mouth as she struggled with the German's self-promotion. The diplomat was quick to notice a slight tremor through her, a feline response that had acknowledged his presence without turning her head. Her awareness of him quickened his pulse. It was the response of an animal readying itself for the chase, a built-in caution that also provoked the chase. Close-up, her radiance was even more startling, and the fine lines around her intense blue eyes suggested a student's dedication, the constant study of a musical score no matter how familiar it might be. When he joined their conversation, she did not alter her posture—as if to declare that he had been part of their discussion all along. He offered a more definite form of the language that had been caught between their different fluencies to dissolve their confusion as it also nullified the younger man's gambit. To dismiss him, for Adela quickly turned her back on him and faced the diplomat, taking him in for the first time. "Now what?" she asked good humoredly to signal the success of Simpson's suave ploy. Her small laugh was knowing and played into a deeper register.

The diplomat made the required small talk, complimenting her playing, her interpretation of the music—all of which she shrugged off delicately as the familiar gab encountered at the buffet table. He could see the sparkle in her eyes beginning to grow dull when he introduced himself as the embassy's cultural affairs attaché, temporarily assigned and in town for only a few days. Her eyes shuttered, then opened with a different focus in them. She was not inexperienced and understood what he was—what he did—but by then his hand had closed firmly around her right wrist.

"Where are you taking me?" she asked a little breathlessly. He had abruptly led her through the embassy's kitchen and down some back stairs to the garage. He told her they required a quieter place to talk. "Where are we going?" Delight turned within the semblance of alarm in her voice as he settled her into one of the limousines. It was some kind of prank, the sequence in a fairy tale she had just encountered in the frigid milieu of Finland, and her feet pattered the car's floor with a schoolgirl's anticipation. She had become curious and fascinated by her own attraction to this ordinary-looking man, as if she were being swept away by the secretary of the local Rotary club—she supposed Helsinki had a Rotary club—and this odd fantasy teased her excitement a little, so she laughed to herself. The men she had known were all of the same cut, catalog handsome and meticulously cultured. They were satisfactory lovers; she had no complaints, for they had been correctly rehearsed in the mechanics and operation of a woman's pleasure. So what she had anticipated to be a prosaic adventure— not unappealing in its novelty—was revealing itself too late as something quite unusual. Simpson was not what she had supposed. He was, in fact, a little threatening. She had already guessed his real work, and now she was conscious of a scent about him, a pungency and a smoldering that were both attractive as they were off-putting.

He had driven them to a small commercial hotel near the railroad station, and her expectations so far were not challenged. But in the room as he methodically removed her clothing—the shifting of trains outside the window—unfastening this item or pushing another aside in an order of his own devise that ignored her preference, she understood the gravity of his difference from other men. The insight flooded her with a liberation that made her lightheaded. Earlier in the evening she had controlled the feelings of several hundred people, and now she had become an instrument herself.

In the dim light of the room, Simpson tried to make out the tattoo that decorated her lower spine just above the cleavage of her buttocks. He assumed it was the youthful ensign from some rebellious campaign in Southern California, where she had grown up and still lived. It resembled the spread wings of a bird—the old Prussian eagle came to mind—as he prepared her for his usage. Face down and her hair undone and entangled in the redundant luxuriance of the silk chemise he had left her to wear, her voice was muffled as she called him a bastard. Then, "you bastard," as if he had betrayed her in some way; she sounded hurt that he had deceived her, that he was not what he had seemed to be. Familiar charges for Simpson to hear, though in different circumstances. He employed her ruthlessly and with no care for her gratification; yet, she had slipped into a kind of trance that resembled rapture while a part of her mind attempted to copy the sensation to reproduce it in her music.

"*Bête*," she cried out, then, "*bête, bête—bête*" in time with his effort until she roiled in his grasp, hissing, "scoundrel."

The archaic language amused him as he contemplated the tattoo above the swell of her behind; words called up perhaps from a school play just at that moment, a scrap of innocence raised in a theatrical defense against him. His hands smoothed the bony articulation of her back as if to stretch the ribs apart, and the image of those juvenile theatrics cued by his brutal method sparked his own release.

When they dressed and restored themselves, they did not speak, though she mentioned she was hungry. She hadn't eaten before the concert. He knew a place of overstuffed divans and discreet table lamps with a late kitchen that served reindeer steaks, fried potatoes, pots of caviar, and buffalo grass–flavored vodka.

"As I said, I'm returning to the States in two days," he told her as they settled into the cushions.

"Our flight is at noon," she countered. Her appetite pleased him. She had spread caviar on a slab of potato like jam on toast. "You're not suggesting that we do this again?" Her laughter was mordant and a little rueful. He had caught her out, found something new in her that she had never suspected, and therefore had a claim on her. "I don't know if I even like you," she continued, cutting her steak. "Like what you do," she added and dabbed her mouth with the napkin. "In any event, 'I find this frenzy insufficient reason / For conversation when next we meet.'" She had regained her balance. He could visualize her coolly reordering a music score on its stand after some of the pages had slipped awry.

"But you don't dislike everything about me," he said. She looked sullen and shrugged but continued cutting up the meat into pieces and then arranging them on the plate in some order of their consumption. "I am basically very kind," Simpson continued, "and good hearted. I won't insult you with feeble phrases about your music. The passion of it and so forth. Your vibrant attack and so forth. I will cite the curve of your neck as you bend over the cello. Intent and serious and vulnerable. I will talk of that. Yes, I want to do this again."

Pelus half listened to him, still a little dismayed that she would be sitting with this man in the middle of the night in Helsinki, this man she would not normally look at twice. Still resonant with his lovemaking, she felt a little drunk, and she had yet to taste the vodka.

Simpson had continued to talk evenly—how their different schedules made regular meetings impossible. The trio was to play in Brussels next week, she told him with an eagerness that momentarily shamed her. That would not work for him, he told her, but the trio's other performances could bring them together, and the calculation of this scheduling caught her fancy. The idea of him waiting in future audiences for her to lay down the cello and give herself to him had an appeal she found appalling but undeniable. Simpson noted the alarm in her eyes and changed the subject.

"The phrase you used about being insufficient reason for conversation—that's not your language."

"No. Edna St. Vincent Millay." She sipped some vodka.

"I'll trade you a quote. Not exactly a quote but an anecdote. Chekhov once advised a young playwright that if he hung a gun over the mantel in the first act, the gun had to be used before the final curtain. The audience would be held in suspense. The tension became a factor in their involvement in this suspended violence, in their pleasure." He settled back in the divan and observed her.

Finally, she turned to him, her profile in shadow. "You really are a scoundrel, aren't you?" she said almost gaily, happy with the confirmation. She thumped him on the chest and then pressed her hand against him, over his heart, and kept it there just a little too long for the gesture to escape its melodramatic nature. It was her manner he was to come to know. His repute in the Foreign Service rested on his ability to sort the genuine from the false, and if playing a role, he reasoned, eased her acceptance of him, then he was content to give her histrionics free rein. She had returned to her supper, her posture militant on the sofa. He sipped some vodka and nibbled a piece of potato that was still crisp and warm. In a far recess of the café, a violin had begun to play a gypsy melody. Adela stiffened and flung down her silverware.

"I was afraid that would happen," she said. She pulled at his sleeve. "We must go. I cannot abide such music."

"It's just a bit of schmaltz to go with the atmosphere."

"No, no." Her mind had been made up unalterably. "I will not listen to such music—it is an abomination. I am going." She had risen and stood before him expectantly, her hand offered. The music neared them, and then the violinist appeared from behind a thick column. His face was contorted over the violin by the certainty of his performance's effect, but Adela continued to waggle her fingers, her determination to flee undiminished. Simpson threw some euros on the table—he always paid in the local currency—and escorted her from the place.

The streets were empty as he drove to the Cumulus, where the trio stayed. She lay against him, her face pressed into his arm, and though just a short distance, she had fallen asleep when he pulled up before the hotel. She fished through her purse and then extracted a card for the trio's agency, telling him they would provide him information about their schedule.

Over the next year, they met several times, each occasion schooling their sensualities, each lesson an exploration of this attraction, both of them trying to understand it. Adela became even more naked in these rented rooms as she unveiled items from her history—if indeed it was her history and not a fable created for herself. In the hours before dawn, she would present him a picture of herself as a girl, her feet barely touching the floor, practicing and practicing, trying to play a Bartok she confessed to him, her face winningly pressed into his neck, she had yet to master. Subtly, he drew her from one story to another—debuts and ravishments, broken promises and goals achieved. She had a degree in philosophy and had been a finalist for a Rhodes Scholarship, but the athletic requirement had stumped her. He gave her only the minimum essentials from his file, and she asked for nothing more. Sometimes, he suspected some of her flamboyant recitations were meant only to restore him.

In Toronto, the trio played their last performance of the season. Simpson had accompanied a trade commission that was to finalize certain agreements on wheat exports. The Conti gave a program of Brahms trios that made the audience demand more than one encore and forced the young women to beg for their release. Afterward in the hotel room, the room service cart pushed to one side, she began to weep as they made love, and she told him of how her stepmother had forced her into a relationship with the woman's lover—she was yet a child—and how a particular allegro in the Brahms reminded her of that cruel ecstasy in her past. "You give me room to breathe," she told Simpson dramatically and pressed herself to him.

Once more, he could not tell how much of this story was true or just drawn from some deep pretense in her being that, like the other tales, she found necessary to reenact in his arms, and he wondered if these histories nourished the sounds she had drawn from her cello that evening. Whether she loved him, as she protested, or loved the operatic drama of their affair was a distinction that had become unimportant.

Simpson knew he loved her and, already lost and damned, he accepted the cost of this captivation, sometimes with a palliative of kisses along one thigh. In a later concert, during her interpretation of a Franc *rondeau*, tears filled his eyes, and he sobbed out of control as the audience had risen around him cheering and whistling. He could not stand, for he had been afraid of her searching him out and their eyes meeting. He could not confront her eager anticipation. Her music had called up all of his offenses and held them against the virtue of her dedication. His assault had gone far beyond the physical, and he kept low in his seat and crept out through the crowd and did not go to her, but sent a message that he had been called away unexpectedly.

It was after the Toronto concert—the Brahms program—that Adela sent him the key to her cottage in Laguna Beach overlooking the Pacific. Of course, he wondered how many other men had a similar key to the kitchen door, but she was scrupulous in cleaning up clues, if there were any, and he always gave her warning when he would be coming through. The back porch contained a bicycle and a bucket and a mop—these two housekeeping items rather touching, he thought—and stacks of newspapers and magazines bundled for disposal. The kitchen was neat and sensibly arranged, colorful potholders on a hook above the stove. Often she would be in Los Angeles when he arrived, rehearsing the next season's offerings, so he moved around the empty rooms, making an inventory of her current reading, assessing the nature of her mail, the bills readied to be paid. He was tempted to read her mail, for by now his passion for her was all consuming, but he pulled back to grant himself some integrity, though he felt his discretion might only be another means of his control over her. He could read her mail or not. The bed would be freshly made, and he would pull the shades, undress, and stretch out in the crisp luxury of the sheets. The fatigue of his travels, usually across several time zones, would seep into his consciousness.

The intimate sounds of her carefully moving about the place would slowly draw him awake. A dresser drawer pulled open and shut. Some water run in the tidy kitchen. A hanger adjusted in the closet. Once, he was awakened by the padding of her fingers against the cello's board as she soundlessly worked through a score in the front room. He lay in bed and viewed her partly from the rear, through the doorway, as she bent over the instrument silently fingering what seemed to be an intricate passage. She repeated the measure over and over. She had changed her clothes and wore the blue silk kimono he had brought her from Hong Kong, and as she embraced the cello, the gown fell away from her naked legs. He relished this mute rehearsal that almost equaled in its intensity anything she played in concert. He wished he could draw her like that, like a Bonnard, one of those arrested images of a woman performing an ordinary task and becoming a sublime figure in doing so. But no such transformation was necessary here, for Adela Pelus was already splendid in her concentration. The weight of his transgressions fell upon him once again, the simple faith he knew in his mother's kitchen now soiled, as the discipline of the musician's innocent practice took measure of the deceit that had become his life.

"Ah, there you are spying on me again," she suddenly said. She placed the cello in its stand, rose, and turned toward him. The kimono fell open as she reached up to loosen her hair. Her lingerie was rather gaudy, nothing he had given her.

That night she prepared tuna steaks quickly seared in sesame oil, and they drank ice cold Muscadet as the sun fell into the Pacific. They made love in the long twilight that is peculiar to the seashore, and several times he let her be the aggressor before bluntly retrieving the role in a final definition of his authority. Around midnight, she led him to a small café on the water's edge that seemed frequented by surfers, and he felt a little out of place, uncomfortable in his hard shoes and buttoned down shirt. Here he told her that he and his wife had been talking about a separation. This fine woman had finally added up all his truancies to make a sum she could no longer factor. He caught a sad moue on Adela's mouth, and she turned a little away from his kiss, a little too quickly began to talk about the trio's difficulties. Their music had become lost in Chicago, and they had had to improvise a program that received rave reviews. Also the violinist had been ill and was not playing her best, and the three of them were unhappy about their management and were looking for another agency to represent them.

Never mind that his many assignments had twisted awry the civil life he and his wife had decently practiced; Adela felt she was responsible for this estrangement. She had hurt a woman she did not know, would never know, and what had begun as a lark, an accidental misstep, had shown itself to be the tawdry offense it might be. Simpson sensed her feelings, though she had tried to cover them with the narrative of the trio's problems, and he traded humdrum samplings with her. The air-conditioning in the hotel in Qatar had broken down, and engineers from a US destroyer that happened to be in port repaired the system. His flight from Sydney had been delayed because of a supposed terrorist threat. The quality of the food in Bangkok had deteriorated.

At last, they fell silent, seemingly content to observe the café's activity, but both had become awkward, as if they were strangers, oddly coupled by some tour package. The bargain he had made with the deity who ruled his success had now included her, and she knew it. But neither could pull away; he could not give her up. She had begun to watch a woman in the corner pick up a guitar, but Simpson was sure she had just come to the same finding and was sorting through the various contingencies. The guitarist picked through an inoffensive refrain that pulled them together once again, and they felt the tenderness that survivors of an accident are said to feel for one another. Later a huge moon silvered the ocean below her cottage, heartbreakingly beautiful in its luminous indifference.

Then, once more he lets himself into her small house and sets his backpack down in the kitchen. The place smells clean, accented by her fragrance. It looks like she has given a dinner party, dishes and glassware rest in the Danish drying rack. In fact, she has warned him that she is having some other friends in for a small supper this evening, and they have been carefully selected for their discretion. His whereabouts would not be revealed; he isn't supposed to be back in the country. The business in Afghanistan has been settled more quickly than expected, and his flight hastily arranged and no less arduous.

The cello greets him from its stand in the living room. He guesses she might be shopping for the evening's meal, and he has a quick image of her choosing the cheeses, flirting a little with the shopkeeper as she tests a St. Andrew triple cream or a pecorino toscano. He lowers the shades in the bedroom and quickly strips. The sheets are fresh, and he stretches between them contentedly. He is back once again, and she will be still his for a time. He stretches his arms as if to encompass the promise of her. His right hand slips under the pillow that will be hers, already anticipating the weight of her head. He feels the gun.

Without looking, he knows the weapon is a small .25-caliber automatic; he can visualize it in his grasp. And it is a pretty little gun when he holds it up, almost feminine and of efficient configuration, silvery, with ivory handles. He weighs it, holds it above his head loosely after he checks the safety. The best safety on a gun, he remembers the marine who had given him a quick course in gun handling saying, is to keep your finger out of the trigger guard. Simpson tests the resistance of the trigger. Why does she have a gun? Her house is isolated, and maybe there have been reports of prowlers. He presses the muzzle to his forehead, then lightly tongues its open barrel and finally holds it against his left nipple. Maybe he is the threat, creeping into her bed. He is the prowler. He is tempted to slip off the safety, just for a moment, just for a little. But then he lowers the weapon and slips it back under the pillow. If punishment is to come, it will not come from his own hand; that would not be a punishment so much as one more caper, another conceit. If he is to be delivered, it is to be her assignment; he is sure of that, and with this certainty in mind he falls asleep.

The story of Bill Schoonmaker, the town clerk of a small town near Albany, New York, is quite different. He was a popular man. The cemetery next to the Dutch Reformed Church was peopled by his ancestors, some of them going back before the Revolution, and this lineage gave him a stature that few could match, as it contributed to his political success. He was reelected to his office over and over, and newcomers considered him a character, a quaint attribute to the old farmhouses they bought and fixed up as vacation retreats. They would tell stories to their friends about him during their winter's calendar in the City, his penchant for striped shirts and leather bow ties, of how he worked out deals for them with county bureaucrats. They could call Bill Schoonmaker from the City, and he would see that the town road crew would have their driveways plowed out for a Christmas holiday. They also told of his involvement with a summer intern.

Her name was Ginny Barker, and her father was the local veterinarian; her mother had gone to Florida. One afternoon in April, Schoonmaker had looked up from his desk in the town hall—he had been reviewing some property deeds—to discover her standing almost timidly outside his doorway. How long she had been there, quietly watching him, he did not know, but he sensed he had been under observation for some time. She had waited for him to notice her. The guidance counselor at the high school had told her to inquire about an internship that was available. The town clerk's office was shorthanded since Mrs. Gardener had died, and this girl was about to graduate and needed to make a little money.

"I want to go to New York to study clothing design at Parson's," she told him. The large windows of the outer office had backlighted her, so she appeared in the doorway more of a silhouette at first—a mass of dark hair, slim figure, and slender schoolgirl legs. Her short skirt was bright red with a couple of ruffles around it. Schoonmaker would remember that dress, but she would never wear it again after that first time.

He had never met Doc Barker's daughter, but he had heard the talk about her—he heard about everything that happened in town. Supposedly one afternoon last winter during the blizzard she had entertained several of the road crew in the town garage while the phones heated up with complaints about the snow accumulating in big drifts that made driving hazardous. But sitting across from him, her tomboyish manner confused the flirtatious image of the short skirt, pulled tight to her knees, as if she had suddenly realized it had been a mistake to wear this dress for the interview.

She had good typing skills and knew about computers and spoke with a casual command of the subjects, her voice breaking now and then into an alto register that he associated with the school glee club. She fluffed her hair as she talked, and her eyes were deep brown and unwavering.

"How's your father?" Schoonmaker asked.

"Oh, Dad's keeping busy with kittens and sick puppies." She laughed, and the deeper sound came into play. "Not many big animals for him to take care of these days. Some of the new people are keeping horses, so that might keep him interested."

"And you want to design clothing," he said, reading from the application form she had handed him with a shrug.

"*Haute couture,*" she answered with an emphasized correctness. Then she guffawed and rolled her eyes. "Fashion work. I made this skirt. It's my design. The ruffles." She tugged at the material, playing with the fabric. "It's all I ever wanted to do. I had the best-dressed dolls in Rensselaer County." When she laughed she drew her knees up almost against her chest. Still a child, Schoonmaker thought and looked away.

It should be clear from the outset that the town clerk was a careful and honorable man, and his eagerness to be of service was as much a part of his profile as the sharp point of his nose. He prided himself in his sense of duty. He was proud of his two children, a son in the Marines and a daughter in nurse's training in Albany, and happy with the life he and his wife followed, which seemed governed by an old manual for behavior they may have come upon in the attic of the farmhouse that had been her family's. Talk in town suggested the acreage was to be subdivided by a developer and that the route through the morass of county and state regulations, deed restrictions and rights of way, had been skillfully guided by the town clerk. Some credited Edna Schoonmaker's family holdings for her husband's grace as he eased around the high counter of his front office to tend to a taxpayer's complaint.

That evening he told his wife about Doc Barker's daughter applying for the internship, and she repeated some of the gossip about the girl as she served the chicken and green pea casserole. "I thought it best to clean out the pea patch before it got too warm," she told him to explain the casserole.

"The peas have been plentiful this year for sure," he answered as he spooned out the food onto his plate. The ice tea was poured, and store-bought rolls were already on the table. Only one place had been set.

"When you're done," she told him, "clean up and put the dishes in the dishwasher and turn it on. I have my club tonight."

"That's right, it's Thursday," Bill Schoonmaker said. "I had forgot."

Edna's club was a group of local women who practiced shooting at targets on a range offered them by the Copake Corners Rod and Gun Club. Bill Schoonmaker had helped their pistol permits ease through the county sheriff's office, and every Thursday evening these women, mostly housewives, some even grandmothers, would step up to the bench, their ears encased by large leather muffs, and blast away at targets fifty yards distant. They resembled a curious militia called up as a last defense against a threat yet to be defined, but there had been some talk recently about prowlers and minor pilfering of sheds and outbuildings in the more remote areas of town. The women always brought their own baked goods and spent much of the time drinking coffee and eating and milling current gossip. Edna Schoonmaker's sticky buns were a favorite.

After he finished his dinner and started the dishwasher, Bill Schoonmaker sat down in the rocking chair on the back porch. He enjoyed these lengthening spring evenings when the tide of shadows gradually claimed the outlying reach of the old fields. Fields of ancient history, he would muse, where Mohawks and settlers—some his ancestors—patrolled the boundaries of his imagination. James Fenimore Cooper had been his favorite reading as he grew up, because he could verify those romances with his own family's history. Good against evil and the force of truth overcoming greed and vanity—everything in those novels played out before him in the twilight as the dishwasher ground behind him. And then he thought of that girl in his office this afternoon—Ginny Barker. The way she fluffed her hair as she talked so earnestly of her plans, the light of ambition that flashed in her dark eyes, and that charming awkwardness with her legs, how to cross them, arrange them in the chair. It had been the innocent posturing of a child playing an adult. He could help her out, help her out of the village calumny that threatened to overwhelm and drag her down. Maybe he would come to her defense.

Whether her behavior had been a practiced flirtation or a guileless attempt at sophistication was irrelevant, because the effect on him had been the same and unmistakable. Warning flags had gone up. He could envision his carefully ministered probity smashed to smithereens and the respect passed across the high counter of the town clerk's office becoming dulled and featureless—all in the flash of a single moment that crossed the line. This afternoon, the urge to reach out and pat one of the pretty knees that anxiously rubbed against each other was mixed with the urge to use his importance to put her on the right track. To put her under his guidance in the town hall could be of greater satisfaction than whatever the louts on the highway crew may have claimed. Schoonmaker congratulated himself for this insight as well as recognizing the inherent danger of such a mission, for try as he might, he could not completely dissolve the images the gossip had provoked. He had seen pictures of such things. Earlier in the year, the state police had used his office to assemble and review evidence from a search of a couple's home—they operated a nursery and landscaping firm—that revealed them to be purveyors of child pornography.

Night had completely obliterated the view from the back porch. Birds had fallen silent. He decided to help Ginny Barker out. She could work under his direction, and that would give her some protection. He could do more. Didn't the two men who bought the old Talcott place have some kind of connection with the fashion business in the City? Schoonmaker understood the nature of their relationship, and their overly tasteful renovation of the plain farmhouse had amused him. But maybe the connection would help her, a step-up, and it would be a confidence between him and the girl. He closed the kitchen door and considered something on television.

For her part, Ginny Barker quickly figured out the nature of her relationship with the town clerk and readily complied. She dressed in slacks and shirtwaists and during the really hot spells wore loose-fitting capris that came well below the knee. Her blouses were similarly roomy and sometimes held at the waist by a bright scarf. Quickly they were on a first-name basis, and he began to anticipate her voice calling him after she answered the phone in the outer office. "Bill, it's Mrs. Connor about her neighbor's dog."

The town clerk's office had never looked so orderly. Ginny kept the files up to date, the minutes of the town meetings neatly retyped and put in folders, the complicated amendments to zoning laws assigned their proper place in one of the cabinets against the back wall of the outer office. Her desk was almost bare save for a note pad and several pencils and the telephone she answered in that throaty register. "Bill, it's Rick Masten reminding you of your appointment to review the plans for his development."

Sometimes after the phone rang, he would listen to her engage in a long conversation with the caller before handing the person over to him. Her voice would sound knowledgeable, familiar with the taxpayer and the problem—often breaking into quick sympathetic laughter—and he would feel a curious pride. Finally when she put him on the line, the person had been prepared by a kind of foreplay that would ease the complaint into Schoonmaker's attention. She had become known to callers, citizens with a problem.

Gradually they became a team and even ate lunch together, the front door of the town hall closed and locked—office hours posted in her squarish, schoolgirl hand. He ate the grilled cheese sandwiches sent over from the Town Diner as Ginny unwrapped several small packages of her own lunch. Usually she brought a container of yogurt, some grapes and carrot sticks, and placed them carefully on a piece of paper towel spread over a corner of his desk. Sometimes she brought tuna salad on a toasted bun and cut a portion of the sandwich for him, insisting he eat it. Dividing the fare, she would bend over him as he remained seated, and her moist aroma would rise from the open neck of her blouse.

"I came by your office today," Edna mentioned at supper one night. "I thought you might want to have a bite with me, but the front door was locked."

"I was there," he told her. "You should have knocked. I was in there, having my lunch. A little peace and quiet."

"I guess that must be a new policy," his wife said and poured them coffee.

"I guess it is," Bill Schoonmaker replied and laughed a little.

Ginny's efficiency filing and sorting papers allowed her to finish her daily tasks quickly, and she spent the rest of the day sketching on a large drawing pad she carried with her everywhere. She sat at her desk at the rear of the front office and drew elaborate gowns and stylish pants suits, sometimes using a whole page to detail several versions of a shirt collar or the cuff of a jacket, the fall of a skirt. Boots and belts. Over and over, her careful drawings would picture, then redefine, an accessory, and Schoonmaker would admire her industry, the single-minded dedication to her ambition. This zeal made her even more interesting, so when the images of their first meeting would come to him, all naked legs and nervous flutter—one finger tracing a line down her throat as she talked—he would be reminded that those features still lay beneath the clothing and competency that clothed her now.

It amused him to think of them as an alliance going about the town's business, driving to a new subdivision to review a drainage field, checking the rodent control at the town dump. Townspeople got used to seeing them turn out of the town hall parking lot in Schoonmaker's SUV on their way to an area of the town that required his inspection. Sometimes, the intern wore dark glasses that made her look older, even mysterious, and he would have to remind himself she was his charge, a young girl who had placed herself under his care and supervision. When he left her at the office to make these rounds by himself, she would assume responsibility for the town's business with a merry zest, and at the building site a foreman would ask, "Where's Ginny?" Then before he left, the man would also say, "Give my best to Edna."

So there were signals, but Schoonmaker convinced himself he was doing no wrong—he hadn't put a hand on the girl—but at the same time he enjoyed the flattery of these intimations. Making the rounds of a new water district with Ginny sitting beside him in the SUV gave him a lift he could not ignore, though it made him wary at the same time. Their joint enterprise exhilarated him as it also made him nervous, and he would check the angle of his bow tie in the rearview mirror to be sure it was exactly parallel to the ground.

The girl had begun to wear her hair pulled back, and as the summer warmed, she wore flip-flops, and even these came off as they drove along. She wore jeans or long shorts or one of her own handmade voluminous skirts that would balloon about her and would have to be trapped between her legs as they sped along a back road. She kept up a running chatter about her father, her mother working in Florida, who was seeing whom in her crowd. Did he think these colors went together okay? "Oh my, I must be Miss Stinky-Poo," she said one morning, sniffing herself. "I ran out of deodorant."

She had leaned across the seat as he drove and raised an arm to present her naked armpit for his inspection. The town clerk looked quickly and then back to the road, just as a car went by, going toward town. It was Mary Thompson on her way to market.

Toward midsummer, the phone rang one morning, and he heard Ginny speak briefly and then announce, "It's a Mr. Elliot Holland." Schoonmaker couldn't place the name, couldn't fit it into the roll of voters he routinely reviewed, and the mannered voice in his ear was very different from the local sound.

"We're just up for the weekend to ready our little estate for summer," the man said, "and if you can put aside your management of the town's destiny, we would love to have you and your charming assistant over for tea. Say about four-ish."

It was the fellow in the garment business, Schoonmaker finally identified the caller, the man he had written about Ginny's ambitions. He checked his calendar and quickly accepted the invitation. His heart was vibrating in his chest as he jumped up and went out to the front office. Ginny was bent over the large drawing pad.

"We've just been invited for tea." His voice startled her. "The guy in the garment business I told you about. I hope you can go—around four."

"I'll have to go home to change," she answered.

"I think they're pretty informal," he said. "Just us and the other guy he apparently lives with."

"Oh my," the girl said, prettily fanning her fingers over her lower face. "Like that, you mean."

"Bring your drawings," Schoonmaker told her quickly.

Schoonmaker was surprised that the city man's house was the same as when he had visited a year before to register him for an absentee ballot. The interior was sparse and apparently the newcomer preferred the stark exposure of the house's post and beam construction and its white plaster walls. A sofa and two armchairs covered in a bright floral print and several ladder-back chairs were the only furniture in the living room. Long blooms of forsythia shot up from a heavy glass vase next to the fireplace.

Ginny had changed into an orange shift that left her arms bare and that, even in its straight lines, still suggested her shape within the garment.

"Love that color," the younger man who had greeted them at the back door said. He had led them through the kitchen and what was the dining room and into where they now sat in the living room. He moved back and forth with a whippetlike grace to serve them from what Schoonmaker recognized as one of the assembly tables from the old clock works. There were tea and a bottle of white wine in a ceramic cooler and some kind of Chinese dumplings he said he had just whipped up. A spicy sauce went with the dumplings, and Ginny knew its name.

"Yes, I think orange is an interesting color but has to be used carefully—not for everyone, I suppose," the girl said, looking at the very heavy man who reclined in one of the armchairs. Elliot Holland nodded wisely.

"So good of you, Bill," he addressed Schoonmaker, "to introduce us to Miss Barker. The fashion business is desperately needful of fresh ideas." He took a glass of wine from his companion.

"And I expect you made what you're wearing," the younger man said amiably.

"Oh, it's just something I whipped up," Ginny replied and laughed and blushed. She had used the man's same wording for his dumplings. "A variation of something I saw in a magazine."

"It's that hint of the Empire here at the waist"—Robert lightly touched his chest—"that teases the line of the bosom."

"Quite so," Elliot Holland agreed. "Well, down to business," he said gaily. "Let's see your portfolio."

Ginny handed it over to him, and he began slowly turning its pages. Robert had come behind him, teacup in hand, to look over his shoulder.

The two men became silent as they studied the drawings. Once, Holland hummed at something, and Robert said, "Yes. Exactly. I agree."

Schoonmaker drank some of his tea and noted Ginny's poise as she followed this inspection. She held the crystal goblet of wine at eye level, and two brightly colored bracelets clattered down her slender arm. The town clerk considered momentarily that she was underage and that he was the so-called responsible adult present, and he was condoning her drinking, and then he chided himself for his rectitude. The four of them seemed very comfortable together—Robert and Holland had offhandedly put them at ease—and if any infraction was incurred, it was probably his own careful behavior.

At supper he tried to tell Edna about the afternoon and what looked like a very successful interview. The two men had praised the girl's ideas, her attention to detail, and Schoonmaker was certain the meeting would lead to something important for Ginny Barker's future. "She really held her own," he told his wife. "Talking about different materials and other designers. When these guys talked about people in the business, she knew the names, knew why they were important." He pictured her holding her glass up for a refill without looking or interrupting her description of a style. It was a gesture she must have learned from the movies. "She really knows her stuff," he told Edna proudly.

"I'm sure she is very grateful to you," his wife said and passed the cole slaw.

What he didn't tell Edna was how he drove the girl home. She had drunk too much wine, and they left her old VW in the town hall parking lot. She had insisted she was okay, but he worried if she had any scrape, he would be responsible for her condition.

But it was more than the wine. The sophistication of the two men, their particular living arrangement, seemed to affect Ginny, and she had become artlessly animated. A sudden, juvenile expression, spoken or displayed, within the put-on ensemble of worldliness made her especially endearing. She was getting drunk, and he had pushed them out the door, though the two men had begged them to stay.

Robert and Holland had made a great fuss over them as they left, and their amusement was scarcely contained within their urbane manner, so the town clerk had speculated momentarily about their sincerity when they praised the girl's work. Yes, they had invited her to contact them in New York, and, yes, they would introduce her into the business. One of their dear friends was in the administration at Parson's.

"You and Ginny must come back again, Bill," Holland said as they passed through the back door. "Maybe we can have supper."

"Oh, yes, absolutely," the younger man agreed. "Thoroughly enchanting," he whispered into Schoonmaker's ear. He widened his eyes and gripped the town clerk's shoulder. Schoonmaker was aware of the congratulatory note in the man's voice, and as he started the car, he considered that the two men had looked on them as a couple—made them a couple—and the designation flattered him, and then he was worried that it had flattered him.

When he turned off the highway and onto the back road that led to the kennels and the veterinarian hospital, Ginny suddenly looked alarmed and began to heave, one hand over her mouth. Schoonmaker quickly braked as she opened the door and fell to her hands and knees to the ground. The town clerk had raced around the car to her as she vomited. He held her up, one hand pressed against her forehead and his other arm around her waist, a hand pressed against her surging belly. He noted the childlike slenderness of her torso was contradicted by the fulsome weight of her bosom as she leaned against him. He looked around; the road was deserted.

"It's all right, it's all right," he soothed her, but she didn't seem embarrassed. Actually, she was laughing and looked sidewise at him as he wiped her mouth and chin with his handkerchief. She offered up her mouth for his attention.

"Well, okay," she said at last and jumped into the car. When he slipped behind the wheel, she had settled into the corner of the seat, holding her soiled dress in a bunch on her lap. Her legs were bare and slack.

"I haven't been to your dad's place in a long time," he said. "It's back in here, isn't it?"

"Yes, back in here and back in here," she said airily. "So much back in here as to be"—she paused to find the word—"really back in here." She giggled and stretched. "I am so very grateful to you, Bill—Mr. Town Clerk Bill. Meeting Elliot Holland and his friend but also—also. Do you realize what you have done for me, Mr. Town Clerk?" She had abruptly risen to kneel on the seat. She faced him, and her dark eyes were fierce. "You have made me—no, not important. I'm not important," she told herself and hiccupped and shook her head. Schoonmaker worried she might throw up again, and it would be all over him, which reminded him he must wash out his handkerchief before he threw it into the laundry basket at home. She was leaning over him, and anyone passing them would get the wrong idea. Ginny had cleared her throat. "Not important," the girl repeated, "but worthy. Yes, you have made me worthy, and I am forever and forever grateful. How can I ever repay you, Mr. Town Clerk Bill?"

"Sit down, Ginny. You will hurt yourself." He concentrated on the road. He had come to a dangerous intersection in his life through no design of his making. Her appeal had always been that fierce ambition to pull herself up and away from all the small mindedness and talk—put those things far behind her as she tirelessly sketched on her drawing pad. He was aware she sketched much more than the illustration of a dress design. But the reason for her appeal had changed into something quite different, sitting next to him, and he recognized it for what it was, telling himself that he had seen it coming all along.

"We mustn't cross the line," he said abruptly and mostly to himself, but she had heard him.

"You're right." She raised a finger. "We mustn't cross the line."

A quick turn on the unfamiliar road, and Ginny lost her balance and fell against him. She sprawled on the seat, her head falling into his lap, the rest of her—arms and legs—scrambled like a doll with its strings coming apart.

"We are in dangerous territory," he told her. He talked about their responsibilities—her important responsibility to herself, her future that waited for her in the City. Yes, he may have arranged for that future, but she had to make it work. He kept talking, hoping her house would appear around the next bend. Whether she heard him or only feigned unconsciousness he could not tell. The weight of her head on his thigh began to hurt, and her mouth had fallen open, and he could look down into its pink interior, into the gap of her throat.

Luckily her father was not home, and only the barking of several dogs greeted them. The noise roused her, and she quickly opened the door and jumped out, holding up her dress with one hand as she tucked the black portfolio under the other arm. She said nothing and walked purposefully up the front steps and into the house without looking back or saying anything. Schoonmaker thought she seemed angry, but she might only have been embarrassed. Or it could have been both.

"Joyce Cornwall's mother cleans house for Holland and his friend," Edna Schoonmaker said that night at supper. He had not told her about the intern throwing up. "She says they have a king-size bed."

"I've only seen their downstairs," Schoonmaker replied. "I didn't see it."

Ginny Barker gave no indication she remembered being sick that afternoon or anything that had happened on the way to her house. She resumed her duties the next day with the same efficiency, and their joint attention to town business continued seemingly unchanged. Sometimes she brought a tuna fish sandwich to share with him, and they ate their lunch in the side yard of the town hall, in the open. Schoonmaker felt better about eating outside. Sometimes he thought he detected a kind of flippancy in her, and he wondered if she was taunting him. She told him she had visited Elliot and Robert—she casually used their names—to show them new designs several times and that they had invited her to "a gala" where she had met several people from the City who asked her to look them up.

"I really got blasted," she boasted, looking at him slyly. "I had to spend the night. They have this huge bed, but I slept on a pull out."

Eventually, the town clerk and the intern resumed their comfortable routines, and he relished her presence in the outer office, filing deeds and other papers, answering the phone, or bending over the large drawing pad, her face stiffened by concentration. She still accompanied him to sites that required his inspection, and she had gotten on good terms with contractors and citizens alike, which, in turn, pleased him—that he had been able to provide her this stature. One of the councilmen talked to him about holding a special town meeting to hear the proposal of a marketing firm to build a large shopping center adjoining the old battleground where Benedict Arnold was supposed to have deflected the British toward Saratoga and their doom. The proposition was very complicated, for it meant extending the water district at taxpayers' expense and, at the same time, placating a small but articulate group in the Historical Society. The intern had to work late several nights to copy and assemble the different packets of documents required for the councilmen to look over, and she had written and had published in local newspapers the notices required by law. It took time to find a night when all concerned could attend, but Ginny was able to arrange a meeting hour agreeable to all.

Schoonmaker usually chaired such meetings, and this one went on late into the night because of the high-tech presentations of the lawyers representing the developers and the impassioned declarations by members of the Historical Society. Ginny sat in the front row, right in front of him, and she looked especially pretty and competent, taking notes on the proceedings. She wore slacks and a sleeveless blouse, and her hair was caught up by a blue scarf. Large gold hoops dangled from her ears, and she talked easily with several men from the architectural firm, laughing loudly at something one of them said. Schoonmaker had been unable to hear the joke.

The meeting finally adjourned close to midnight, the different petitions and motions reviewed, tabled, or passed. He helped her put away the paperwork the meeting had created, set the office straight, turn out the lights, and lock the town hall.

"You were wonderful tonight, Ginny," he told her in the darkened parking lot. They stood between their cars. A brilliant moon illuminated the neighborhood, and the white siding of the town hall seemed to reflect and intensify the light, though it made the shadows blacker.

"How wonderful am I, Bill?" She turned to one side and fidgeted with her car keys. "Why do you think I am wonderful? What do I do that's so wonderful?" Her voice coming through the semidarkness seemed to change into the weary sound of an older woman talking. Schoonmaker could not fathom the shift in this schoolgirl, and the transformation frightened him a little. Or was it a transformation? Maybe her true nature had been disguised within the coltish gaucherie she had worn from the beginning? The houses bunched around the parking lot seemed to wait expectantly for their words, that their sound might automatically turn on lights. But Ginny continued to speak quietly.

"What do you want of me?" she asked almost casually. "I can't figure it out. What is it you want? What am I supposed to do? Tell me what to do."

She sounded a little like the time she had been drunk, and Schoonmaker became frightened because she wasn't drunk, and at the same time, her exasperation rang true. He accepted her anger. He had done something to her, he knew that, but for the life of him he couldn't figure out what.

"You have this line we tiptoe around, this side and that side, and you decide where to cross—where not to cross. Excuse me. Have I crossed the line? Am I crossing the line?" She went on her toes and leaned into him to quickly take one end of his bow tie between her lips, pulling and sucking on it. "There," she said releasing it. "Have I crossed the line, Mr. Town Clerk Bill?"

She folded herself into her car gracefully and started it up before he could respond. She pulled out of the parking lot, carefully observing all the traffic signs posted on the deserted intersection, her directional signals flashing almost angrily.

Schoonmaker drove home slowly, turning over the intern's words and her outrageous behavior. He felt his bow tie, still damp, slipped it off and put it in his pocket. He opened his shirt collar. Ginny had scared him just then in the parking lot, but she would be leaving for the City soon, and though he would miss her—he had grown accustomed to her—it was good that this relationship would end by itself, almost naturally.

He had passed the town limits and was in the countryside. The fields on either side were clearly visible in the moonlight, and he turned off the headlights. He often enjoyed driving only by the light of the moon, being extra watchful for deer, and he remembered how, when they were young, he and Edna would often drive home from a social occasion with the car lights off. In winter, the snow on the fields made the countryside as bright as day, and it was comforting, snug even, to move over the darkened landscape in their darkened car, being one with the natural world and not set apart by artificial illumination. One time, again it was winter when they returned from a holiday party, he had the lights off, and they hummed tunes from the car's radio. Edna reached for his right hand and pulled it to herself, pushed it into her lap. Then she raised her skirt and pulled his hand and fingers against the humid junction of her body and held him there, directed his hand. He took his eyes from the road momentarily to look at her. She had half fallen against her seat, her eyes wide open but unseeing, focused on something outside the field of vision. He quickly looked back to the road ahead for deer.

• • •

No lights in the house this night either as he rolled up to the barn and cut off the engine. Tree frogs trilled in the night. He walked around to the back of the house and took in the vastness of the backfields that lay exposed in the silvery light. Ghosts were surely playing in those meadows, and he laughed silently at the idea. Then he approached the back porch and just then a figure stood up, and he was startled. But it was Edna, and she had waited up to greet him. Schoonmaker was immediately joyful as his wife raised her arm and shot him full in the face. He was dead before he hit the ground.

The coroner's inquest agreed with the sheriff's report that it had been an accidental homicide, and no charges were pressed. Edna testified that she mistook him for a prowler and that she had called out a warning but he had kept coming. Bill Schoonmaker was buried with his ancestors next to the Dutch Reformed Church, and the town clerk's office was closed for a week until the school district's bookkeeper was temporarily hired. Edna Schoonmaker went to Sarasota, Florida, after settling with the developer who bought her family's acreage. She was reported to be very happy. She opened a shop that sold jewelry made from seashells. Ginny Barker did go to New York and to Parson's, but after completing two years of superior but not extraordinary work, she disappeared. The gun, a .25-caliber Colt automatic with pearl handles, remained unclaimed in the sheriff's office and was eventually destroyed during a routine procedure meant to demonstrate the community's safety.

The Moving Finger

One time, changing planes at O'Hare, he yields to an impulse. More than once, on other trips, he had looked up her number, had split the thick slab of the Chicago phone directory apart, and traced down the long columns of Joneses to what might be her number. But he had never made the call and spent the time until his next flight prowling the vast terminal.

Jones, C. W. Cynthia Jones. Cindy. He could not remember if her middle name began with a *W* or even if she had a middle name, and so he was not sure if this was the same woman whose long legs and large brown eyes had been among the more comprehensive studies of his senior year. He remembered her forthright manner and the enthusiasm with which she would enter his off-campus apartment, spill her books in the kitchen, and slip out of her clothes in the bedroom, where they raised gentle conspiracies against the establishment.

Jones, C. W. He had heard several years ago she had been through a bad marriage, had lived in Europe, and then returned, divorced, taking back her family name. But the initials stumped him, as they were probably meant to discourage obscene phone calls or maybe even the calls of old lovers passing through town, which might be the same thing. That thought made him pause each time he looked her up and every time close the heavy directory and start a casual inspection of the terminal building.

But something else kept him from tapping the number into his cell phone. Generally, a few hours before, his wife would have driven him to the small town still graced with train service into New York City. It would be early in the morning, and she would have pulled his barn coat over her nightgown, a pair of his boots on her feet. Her mouth would be warm and her body fragrant as they kissed in the parking lot of the station before the train's arrival. Hours later in the filtered impersonal atmosphere of the O'Hare air terminal, he could call up the taste of her lips and was warmed by her aroma rising from the open throat of her gown—half woman's flesh, half warm bed. A phone call to someone in the distant pall that was Chicago, a person who would be no closer afterward, would somehow abuse the sense of separation from his wife that he valued, even relished the melancholy it prompted in him.

So the questionable Jones, C. W.—looked up every time he passed through—was always smothered in the pages of the phone book, and he spent his time looking for the flaw a colleague had told him about, a remote wing of the terminal where its enormous windows look out on a blank wall.

But this time, it is different; a little more than a year has passed since his last layover in Chicago. The weather is rather balmy when he changes planes, and he has about an hour's wait before his flight to Los Angeles. His final destination is Hong Kong. But it was cold at home this morning, and after three days of rain, the SUV would not start. It was probably the fuel pump again, and he had told his wife to get it checked out, but she had not taken the car to the garage; too busy at her own office, she said.

Also, one of the boys was in bed with his foot bandaged, shot full of serum because he had stepped on a broken bottle while playing around the trash burner. All bottles and cans were supposed to have been separated and taken to the town recycling center, never thrown in with the paper and other burnables. He had laid down that procedure several times.

Finally, while shaving, he gagged on the disgusting odor that rose from the sink drain, danger signals sent up by the old cesspool from its undiscovered location. None of their neighbors, natives of the area, could remember where the old farmer who had sold them the house had dug the cesspool—somewhere in the front acreage, but he'd never found it.

But what really has him fidgeting and cracking his knuckles in Chicago was his wife's cool, almost impertinent, response to these problems. If she could not immediately come up with solutions, as with the forgotten cesspool, she seemed to face them down with an insouciance that fit them within a point scale fixed in her mind but strange to him.

As he makes his way to the telecommunication center, he reviews how calmly she called the farmer who rented their pastures. Well, she answered his objection, the SUV wouldn't start—an embarrassment all its own in their hamlet—and there were no taxis. He had to catch a train in Green River that would put him on his way to Hong Kong. Anyway, she added with a maddening assurance, they charge the farmer very little for their pastures, and he would be happy to do this favor for them. So, a few minutes later, he was bouncing on the seat of a pickup truck as the farmer, a man about his father's age, talked agreeably about the weather, backed-up cesspools, and the vagaries of an SUV.

Jones. Jones. Jones. He has a half hour before his plane for LA leaves. Perhaps she has moved since he last looked her up; maybe she has remarried and changed her name. Or she might be working—what would she be doing?—it's eleven in the morning in Chicago. He tries to remember what her major was, what her interests were. But yes—there she is. Jones, C. W. In a different location in the current directory.

"Hello?" Miraculously, it is her voice, no doubt about it. It is the same sound, the same inflection as when she called him late from her dorm room. "Hello?" A little anxiety in her voice now, and he almost cancels the message, but that would make him another heavy breather on the line, one more reason for her anonymous entry. "Oh, hi," she says after he announces himself. Her casual tone evaporates the years since their last conversation. "What are you doing in Chicago?"

"I'm between planes at O'Hare and thought I'd call to say hello."

"Well, hello," she says. He can hear a small dog barking in the background, an urgent sound. "How did you know I'm in Chicago?"

"A while back, I ran into Skip Butterfield . . ."

"Skip who?"

"Skip Butterfield—one of the old gang. I guess you don't remember. Well, no reason to remember him, but he said he had heard you were in Chicago. Well, I just thought I'd give you a call, that it would be fun to say hello. Catch up. I'm between planes."

"Where are you going?"

"Hong Kong."

"Wow, Hong Kong."

"Well, it's on business."

"I see," she says. "I think you were going to be an architect, weren't you?" It sounds as if she has just pulled his card from the file.

"Gosh, you remember. Yeah, that's right." He is suddenly elated that she has remembered that detail, and he turns to look at the newsstand. Men and women are browsing the magazines.

"Are you building stuff in Hong Kong, one of those skyscrapers you see on television?"

"Actually, I ended up in urban planning. I guess my ideas for buildings, houses, were too wild for certain people. But we were lucky on the bidding for this job for the Hong Kong government, and I'm going over to do the groundwork."

"That's nice," she says. "You must be very successful."

"Well, it's a living," he answers and laughs. A guy sitting nearby looks at him over his newspaper, then returns to the article he's reading. The sun is pouring through the huge windows, and he feels his face flush. "What— what are you doing these days, Cindy?"

"Oh, a little of this and a little of that. My mother died. Then I got married. We lived in Majorca. But he was a jerk. So I came back and I went back to my painting."

"Oh, good," he says, not remembering her painting.

"You live in New York City?" she says and speaks off the phone to the dog barking. The dog stops barking, then starts again.

"No, we live upstate, about a hundred miles from the city. It's an old farmhouse we bought three years ago with a little land around it."

"So city life got too much for you and you moved to the suburbs."

"Well, maybe." He returns some of her laugh, good-naturedly. "But actually, it isn't the suburbs, quite rural; it's not all that simple. We're—"

"I find all that curious." Her voice interrupts him. The sound has become flat, and he recalls how she would squint when she became serious about something.

"Ah, what's curious, Cindy?"

"Well, how you can run around planning urban environments for people while you have opted for a rustic setting. I have to do something about this goddamn dog. What's your number? I'll call you back. We have raised certain ethical questions that need to be addressed."

Wonderingly, he finds himself giving her his cell phone number and then walks to the outside window that looks out on the landing field. She was fond of making ethical points, now that he thinks about it. Late at night when all he wanted was a little sleep, she would sit up in bed, full of energy and resolve, raising ethical points.

Perhaps she had taken the number down incorrectly. Or maybe the dog was putting up a fight or a deliveryman had rung her doorbell. A few minutes more and he would be at the gate and have to turn off his phone and he would be free of her. But now she had his number and could call him afterward—anytime. Then something else pops into his mind. Wasn't she—Cindy—the one with the seemingly endless supply of Kahlil Gibran quotations? Whenever she slipped into bed, she would bless their lovemaking with a line or two from *The Prophet*.

His phone rings in his pocket. He could decide not to answer, but he knows it would continue to ring. He knows she wouldn't let up. He would receive strange looks from others waiting for their flights. He imagines her standing patiently in the remote overcast of the city, confident he will answer. She could call him now any time. He punches the speak button.

"I don't suppose you even try to do anything with all that land you own." Her voice has started in his ear immediately.

"Well. There's not a whole lot of it, but we do rent the pasture to a local dairy farmer, a neighbor. In fact, this morning, he gave me—"

"So you make a profit on this land that you don't work yourself."

"The term *rent* is kind of a joke, Cindy. Very little money changes hands."

"So you sit up there in your own private Taliesin like some kind of Count Tolstoy and tell people how to live in the ghetto."

"Now wait a minute, Cindy. Cindy? First, it's just an old farmhouse, falling down when we bought it. Why—," and he almost tells her about the cesspool, but he starts to laugh.

"I find nothing funny about this situation," she tells him. Does that phrase sound familiar? The dog's barking is distant, perhaps from inside her bathroom. "What you're doing would attract my ex-husband. That life you're living. He always wanted to be a gentleman farmer. Never wanted to be involved, to make a commitment."

"That's too bad," he says checking the departure panel. His flight has just flipped into view.

"He couldn't take what I had been saying all along, and then 9/11 proved what I had been saying, and he still couldn't accept it."

"Accept what, Cindy?"

"How it all goes back to Martin Luther King and Bobby Kennedy."

"I'm sorry, but I don't get it." He's certain now she was the one with all the Kahlil Gibran quotes.

"Where have you been?" Her tone is patient, amused. "Don't they get the papers up there on your estate? 9/11 was the culmination of the plot that started back when JFK was killed—all of them led one to the other."

"But who would organize such a plot?" he asks.

"Well, it has something to do with oil, baby. It's how we got into the mess in Iraq today. It's no accident that the guy who killed Bobby was from the oil-rich Middle East. Nor is it any accident that Oswald tried to get a job in the Mexican oil fields. And where was King's assassin captured?"

"Ah . . . Portugal?" he suggests.

"No, he had been there already; he had a ticket for the Middle East."

"I don't remember reading that detail."

"Obviously," she says in a little girl voice. She's about to make another point. "You don't read the right things. You ought to start reading some of the news that doesn't fit. That's unfit. People like you are letting Cheney and company turn the government upside down just to get hold of the oil. That's what 9/11 was all about. You think those guys could fly two big planes into those towers without some help from higher up?"

"Cindy, I'm sorry. I'm really sorry. What happened is awful, and I wish we had more time. I mean not just on the phone but to sit down and talk these things over. Like old times."

"Sure you do," she answers. "Mr. Big Shot on his way to Hong Kong calls up the old girlfriend to give her a thrill, to show her what a big success he is. WILL YOU SHUT UP," she shouts at the dog, and it sounds like she's thrown something at the bathroom door. The dog goes silent abruptly.

"Just zipping through town," she continues, "changing planes so there's no chance of a real meeting, just a phone call. Right? No commitment there." Her voice has grown hard though not completely firm. "I remember that's just like you; claim to want to do something in circumstances that prohibit their doing. That's you, all right. You know how long it takes to get from O'Hare to where I live? Sometimes two hours. Fat chance sitting down to talk things over between planes on your way to big deals. But let's give the old girl a call, cop a feel by way of Ma Bell. You think I'm one of those sex call numbers?"

"Oh, please, please, Cindy, it's not that. That's not the reason I called, believe me." He hears his voice, and he knows he is sincere. The dog has begun yapping again.

"Oh yeah," she comes back dryly. "Then why did you call me?"

"Well, I don't really know," he admits wearily, trying to be honest with himself, trying to recall his reason. Then, he has an inspiration. "Let's just say, 'the moving finger writes, and having writ moves on.'"

She says nothing for several seconds. Even the dog has stopped barking. Then her laughter is painful in his ear. "The moving what? The moving finger? You're the one who needs help, baby. You know what you can do with your moving finger!" The line goes dead abruptly.

Over the sparkling Pacific, still following the sun, he figures he may have been trying to find some kind of fulcrum in Chicago on which to balance his travels, but he would have to look for it elsewhere. As unkempt as the present might be, it is a safer place to explore than old grounds where anything could have happened.

Shoe Polish

Men looking down. Men sitting in chairs and looking down with appreciation, suspended pleasure. Some wryly study the industry at their feet—the meticulous polishing of leather as the bootblack's cloth snaps like a pennant in the wind. Something like a chain of command, too, Anne thought, the men sitting high in the elevated chairs with their feet fitted on the brass supports as the shoeshine bends low over the shoes, smoothing wax into the leather and buffing it to a supple glow. Best of all was the toothbrush dipped in dark stain to limn the crevice where the shoe's sole joins the last. As a child, she always imagined she heard this final flourish accompanied by the ting of a triangle, like the last note of a sprightly Christmas medley played by the Pittsburgh Pops.

So, once again in Pittsburgh, but only passing through this time and momentarily stalled between planes, Anne had idly browsed the glossy strips of stores and food counters laid down on either side of the corridors like tapes of packaged luxuries. At the top of one of these avenues, she had come upon the recessed cubicle, perhaps intended as the foyer to a door-way the architect had forgotten to include in his final drawings. Within it were the two high chairs with two men in them looking down at the two men at their feet whose arms and hands moved in unison, a duet in a sort of scherzo, a dashing 4/4 rhythm. She paused, waiting for the final touch, and, just then one of the shoeblacks did run a toothbrush around each shoe before him, then tossed the brush into an old coffee can beneath the chair. Ever so slightly, he tapped the sole of his customer's right shoe with one finger, a slight touch but enough to start the man from the chair who stepped quickly down to the floor, looking a little embarrassed by what had just happened. He peeled off some currency, handed it over, picked up his briefcase, and walked away, never looking back.

Anne also was caught unaware, for the bootblack had been looking at her. Even as he carefully folded up the bills and slipped them into his vest pocket, his eyes had taken her in, a flick of amusement at their corners as his left hand opened and was held out. Next? She hugged her violin and turned away.

The old air terminal, the one she still walked through in her dreams, stood empty across the vast concrete prairie of landing strips, but it could not be seen from any of the new terminal's enormous glass walls that looked out on views only worth watching for a few seconds. But Anne knew it was there. Someone had sent her a newspaper clipping that reported the opening of the new facility and mentioned that the old one might be turned into a museum. "I thought of you," the person had written.

Nothing in this glossy center resembled the cozy improvisation of the old place, other than the airplanes parked just outside its glass walls. The distance between the check-in counters and the new departure gates was so great that a train had been installed to service the space. Though this was a feature she had encountered in other airports, apparently something of a joke passed around by the world's architects, it became a gratuitous insult to the memory of that relaxed, comfortable mode of train travel that has been replaced by the crabbed efficiency of the jet airliner.

Going from window to window, Anne looked in vain for the old terminal, always returning to the enormous reception area and there to stand under the same huge Calder mobile that had mesmerized her as a child. The ponderous delicacy of the sculpture barely moved above her head as travelers passed around her to catch their flights. Here, in the new terminal, the construction hung not in the center of the reception area, but to one side and so close to a wall she wondered if its ungainly limbs might scrape during a heedless turn. Insurance considerations, she speculated, had discouraged its installation in the center, above the information desk, where it could turn freely and unchecked. She walked toward another corridor.

Though that word suggested a passageway snugly fitted to the human figure and perhaps dimly lit, in this new terminal there seemed to be no walls and scarcely a ceiling to these thoroughfares, only the endlessly moving parallel of an automatic walkway to keep the aimless pedestrian on the correct line between two points. How different from the dim warren of hallways in the old terminal, passages that sloped and cornered unevenly, darted up and down, but which somehow got passengers to the correct check-in counter that looked hammered together just as ticket holders appeared. She had known every turn of that building and had returned to it in her dreams with her book bag over her shoulder, her violin case under the other arm, dodging and ferreting out the maze with a bold expertise, a certainty of movement that surely must have been noticed by others. She never got lost, but coming on Mae's Shoe Service always surprised her, as if her mother had magically also set up the small shop just at the right moment and placed it in her daughter's way.

Of course, it never moved from its cubbyhole in one far wing of the terminal—next to a men's room that gave off strong odors of disinfectant and the continuous flush of water. At her own expense, her mother had installed special lighting for the benefit of her customers, most of whom always seemed to be reading thick briefs in small print. This extra illumination flooded the hallway, and its intensity startled people, causing some to pause, pull up their progress as if they had been about to step into the pool of an emergency. Two chairs rose like thrones in the center of the space. Beneath them were the boxy drawers with brushes, cleaners, and different waxes. The small glass-fronted counter stood to the right, holding samples of shoelaces, waxes, and an assortment of toiletries her mother stocked for customers who might have forgotten razors, soaps, deodorants, and lotions in their impetuous departures.

Sitting on top of this counter was the cash register. The embossed brass casing caught the light and returned its glare with the eminence of a holy object.

A rectangular window was at its top and, at her mother's command, the amount to be charged popped into view. For years, Anne had imagined that her mother had taken an old sewing machine and turned it upside down, figuring out some way to have it tabulate the price of a shoeshine. A drawer would pop out from the bottom to receive the money with a merry chime.

Often, she would stand across the hallway, beyond the curtain of light thrown upon the area, and watch her mother at work—bent over, the broad beam of her posterior presented to every passerby, her arms moving like pistons, her hands brisk and efficient. She was a professional. Usually another customer waited his turn patiently in the second chair, reading a newspaper or reviewing business documents—confident his turn would come. Her mother wore a long apron of denim with deep pockets that held a brush or cloths and a small whiskbroom. Her hair was pulled back tightly into a knot to resemble the pictures of her own mother and her mother's mother on the mantel of their living room. Indeed, it was how Anne still wore her hair but with some variations.

From this angle, from across the corridor, she could never see her mother's head or her face but only the sturdy legs, always in slacks, and the solid behind. The constant motion of the arms and shoulders absorbed Anne in a way she could never put into words.

Mae's Shoe Service had many regular customers, men who would chat with her mother as she put their money into the drawer of the ornate cash register. They talked like relatives or even neighbors, because they seemed to know a lot about her and her mother. They would ask about the small garden behind their house, how the tomatoes were doing, or snow tires— what kind would be suitable for their old Dodge? A couple, Anne especially remembered these men, would repeat their military service records, identify their units and campaigns in the war into which her father had disappeared. "There's Annie." One might eventually spot her as her mother helped him on with his coat, whisking the shoulders of it with the small hand broom. "When you going to give us a little concert on that fiddle?"

"She's doing very well," her mother would say, meaning doing too well for a hallway sonata. "She never even plays for me anymore." And everyone would laugh and look at Anne, pleased with her.

Of course, her mother was boasting, not really complaining, and Anne basked in the warmth of her mother's pride, in the near reverence her mother had for her daughter's gift, though she had no understanding of that gift or how it was being disciplined and nurtured by the special classes at the arts school. Anne's mastery of the instrument had gone beyond her mother's hearing, and she had accepted this separation as if it were a natural mystery, like the distant, oncoming light from the stars.

Her mother never put this feeling into words. Certainly not with her customers. But as her mother talked to these men about her, in the bleak brilliance of the alcove's illumination, her expression became serious and knowing, politely prepared to deflect flippant remarks. Her mother stood by the register, before the rack of different-colored tins of shoe polish, which were like an exhibit in an art gallery. Indeed, Anne had just seen such an installation in a museum in Copenhagen. It was called *Shoe Polish.*

More than once, a customer would give them a pass to the executive dining room on the mezzanine of the terminal, and they would have their supper—the bill always discreetly taken care of in advance—on pressed white linen with heavy silverware of so many uses as to make a person wonder how long the meal would take. The white, white tablecloth looked new every time, and its whiteness made Anne cringe a little, because her mother was never able to completely scrub out the stains of the shoe wax from her hands. She wished once that her mother could somehow eat without using her hands, without lifting them from her lap to the table level. The idea caught her and shamed her, so she fiddled with the several spoons beside her plate until her mother told her to stop.

"Living it up, Mae," the waiter always said. He wore a short maroon jacket and a bow tie of the same color.

"Oh, you know how it is, Carl," she would say, and they both laughed like old friends. Early on, Anne had figured that all the people who worked in the terminal, no matter the job, were part of a franchise that was different from their citizenry in Pittsburgh but was just as viable, easier but no less important.

"The veal chop is especially good tonight," Carl would continue— insider's information. "It comes with roasted red potatoes and creamed spinach. And what about a glass of wine? Red or white?"

Her mother always chose red and then smoothed the heavy linen napkin across her lap, beaming across the table. Anne recognized the joy in her face, knew the intelligence behind the happiness that puffed her up. This supper in this exclusive dining room was a reward for a day's work done faithfully and well. Her hands, ceaselessly moving, had provided this treat, this sparkling magical interlude for the two of them, and she lifted the glass of wine to her lips with her small finger elegantly extended.

Today, Anne was pleasantly surprised to see that the bar of the first-class lounge in the new terminal had that Tocai wine from Friuli she had learned to like in Milan last year. A lover had introduced her to its crisp chalkiness along with the Tartini sonata she had made one of her encore selections. Well, yes, he had shown her a few other things, she admitted and checked herself in the mirror behind the bar. She wasn't looking too pleased with herself. But it was somehow right to sip this complex, lovely wine as she called the concert manager to say that her plane was a little delayed and that she hoped this wouldn't cramp the rehearsal time with the orchestra.

"It will not be a problem." His cultured voice sounded in her ear. The consonants of his Nordic accent seemed to have been embellished by his tenure in Denver. "It is just the andante of the Nielsen that we need to go over, and it only takes fourteen minutes or even less if you employ that Stern afterburner you sometimes turn on." He paused to let her relish his cleverness. "As I think I told you, your articulation in London was absolutely brilliant."

"Yes, thank you again."

"Of course, no problem. But one thing, Anne—might I suggest you do one thing?"

"Yes?" The wine was like a dry perfume on her tongue.

"I wonder if you would consider wearing your hair down?"

"Wear my hair down?"

"Yes." He sounded as if he was holding his breath.

"You mean do the bad girl over the Dane."

"Well, yes," he caught himself. "Ha-ha, I mean, well—you are, I mean. It's just a thought."

"I fear you want to package me, Eric," Anne said, holding back a giggle.

"Well," and he did his ha-ha again, "it's just an idea. Whatever you wish, of course."

"I'll think about it," she told him.

But most times, she and her mother would have their supper in the public cafeteria and restaurant in the old terminal after Anne had been dropped off by the school bus or by her violin teacher, Mr. Thatcher. One of the waitresses, a friend of her mother's, would always have a booth empty and ready for them. To walk to this booth at the rear of the restaurant and across from the counter was even better than entering the luxurious setting of the private dining room above. It was a special place reserved for them. Though the plastic placemats on the table and the knife, fork, and spoon rolled into the cocoon of a paper napkin were no different from the other settings, the fact that this booth had been waiting for them, and only them, to slip into its hard, darkly stained wooden seats gave Anne her first taste of celebrity. At the same time, she perceived that the menu of the fancy restaurant on the mezzanine, with the exception of not having hamburgers, was no different from the food served in the cafeteria, so she had also learned how to sensibly evaluate celebrity.

"How're you'ns?" the waitress greeted them as always, plunking down two glasses of water.

"We're just fine. And how are you, Betty?" Her mother leaned forward against the table and looked up, eager for good news. The strong, blunt hands were clasped before her, in a gesture of prayer.

"Well, Geraldine's water broke at four this morning. I just talked with Billy, and he said the doctor said not to worry, that he would be at the hospital, and if her 'tractions started, to call him there. Whatta you looking at? We just ran out of the creamed spinach."

After they had ordered, Anne knew her mother was quietly taking her daughter in, wondering what to say. Anne had not wanted to be a part of the women's conversation and had looked away, retreating into ignorance. After a moment, after taking a sip of water and clearing her throat, her mother told her everything there was to know, so by the time they were served their pie à la mode, Anne had learned everything she would need to know.

"You have your father's hands," her mother said, reaching across the table. "Long, strong fingers." She had taken one of Anne's hands into her own and gently caressed the flesh and then turned it over as if she were going to read the palm. Her mother's hands were supple but strangely firm, not masculine but worn smooth in places creases should have been. Holding hands in public embarrassed Anne, and she had wanted to pull away.

"Yes, I know, darling. Sorry. But I just heard about a new hand cleaner that's supposed to be pretty good. I promise to get some."

No, that wasn't it, Anne had wanted to say, as her mother's hands quickly disappeared from the tabletop and into her lap. "No, that wasn't it," Anne said half aloud as she looked for a seat near a window of the new terminal. She had only been a child, and such public display of affection made her feel even more awkward, though she craved the affection, and the same duality was part of her yet. It even charged her music to ignite her playing with a distinctive passion that was at once cool and full-bodied. That's what Eric had been trying to say in his stiff gallantry.

She wished she had gone to the airline's private club, where she might review the concert's program in a more serene surrounding than this homogeneous waiting area. Children played in frenzies of fatigue as their families talked urgently, to get everything said in time, before parting. Yet, privacy was not always possible in the more privileged area either, where it was more likely someone would recognize her, come forward to say they had seen her play in St. Louis or Paris. Or, just as often, a man would come on to her in one of those ridiculous pastimes some men seem to pursue while waiting for their next flight, when only talk was possible. Some form of safe sex, she suspected, and pretty damn boring.

By the position of the sun, she realized she had taken a seat before a window facing north. Beyond the enormous flatland of the airfield—the tiny toy of a jet liner had just touched down at the farthest boundary—and over the hills rolling into the distance, outside the city limits, her mother lay buried. And next to her was Claude.

• • •

One afternoon, she had rushed through the old terminal, her book satchel and violin hugged to her chest, still thrilling with Mr. Thatcher's news. She had been chosen to solo with the Pittsburgh Pops. The rondo from a Grieg concerto. She must have covered the route through the puzzle of passageways in record time, to round the last corner and come upon the floodlit parentheses of Mae's Shoe Service within the gloomy hallway. She had pulled up short, for something was very different, and she did not immediately know what.

"This is Claude," her mother said simply.

"Hello, Sugar," the man said and held out his hand. The flesh was the color of the dark brown polish used on expensive cordovans, and the palm was large and had a satiny feel when it enclosed her hand. "I'm mighty pleased to make your acquaintance. Your mama does nothing but talk about you."

Anne had tried to say something back, for she had immediately liked his broad, dark face, but her mind was asking the question, how long had this been going on? For she instinctively knew, this instinct refined during that one supper with her mother a few years back, that her mother and this short, burly man had been a couple for some time. Right under her eyes, they had become a pair, and the idea of it quickly appealed to her.

Claude had half owned a shoe shop in one of the hotels downtown, but his partner had died, and because of some legality in the lease, he had lost the concession. Meantime, they had met—Anne wondered sometimes if there was a sort of clubhouse where shoeshine people hung out, talked of different kinds of wax and brushes, for instance—and it seemed perfectly natural for her mother to take Claude into the business. So, it became the two of them, working side by side, both bent over as if they might be passing secrets to each other as their arms and hands worked in tandem over two customers at a time. The cash register chimed with a quickened rhythm, and customers still chatted with her mother about tomatoes and kidded Anne about not playing for them, but they also talked to Claude now, in raised voices, about the Pirates or the Steelers, depending on the season. In fact, Claude wore a Steelers cap at work, set backward on his head with the bill hanging over his thick neck.

"He's a good man," her mother said one evening as if Anne had asked her a question. The relationship had become more than business.

"Yes, I think so."

"He helps me a lot." They had both ordered the Swiss steak with Lyonized potatoes.

"Yes," Anne said.

"He makes me happy." Her mother looked directly into her eyes.

"And that makes me happy," Anne replied. Claude had not joined them for this evening meal; he always brought a sandwich to eat at the stand, saying he could do a dozen shines while they ate, putting more cash into the till. In fact, he never ate with them in the cafeteria, and the invitations to the private dining room had ceased.

What would she say to the one or two friends she could still remember if she called them from the airport, even if she could find their numbers in the phone book? How puzzled, even suspicious they might become to hear her announcing herself after she had left them years ago, after she had taken up her violin and gone beyond the city limits and onto stages far from their girlhoods. The change had been so rapid—the special classes and the scholarships—the abrupt transformation must have mystified them, made them feel she had deceived them, somehow had passed herself off as one of them until her difference could no longer be hidden. And Claude had been important to this transition from schoolgirl to virtuoso, though it would have happened without him, but he had been present. He had been its gentle witness.

He had deftly moved into their life, a casual entry into their intimacy, as he would smile and say, "That's right; that's good." He expanded their small garden to include peppery-tasting greens he cooked with ham hocks she learned to like immensely. When he moved through the rooms of their small house, he gave their space a dimension she and her mother had not been aware they had lacked. And his voice—Anne could still hear his voice, even above the airport's piped music (the "Bolero," sounded like Previn's)—covered them like caramel. At night, she would drift happily into sleep, hearing that soothing tone from the bedroom down the hall.

One night his voice had raised, heavier syrup that poured over the shy sounds her mother made. "It's not right for you now to get yourself soiled. That's what I'm to do. You look after the place and take the money. That's what you're supposed to do. You do the place." Her mother said something, a longish declaration, and he repeated the same lines, not angrily, but with an exasperated tenderness.

On her first weekend home from Juilliard, Anne became aware of the difference that had been foreshadowed by that midnight conversation, and only then, for in the meantime she had lost her own seeing and hearing of anything beyond the score on the music stand before her. She had been caught up in the heat of her own music, a kind of horniness. The simile amused her, because, by then, she had come into this other knowledge. She couldn't quite recall the boy's name, but he played the classical guitar fairly well, and the pads of his fingers had become callused and were exciting to feel upon her. Previn had just brought the Ravel to its smashing climax.

Then, only Claude bent low over the shoes on the brass foot rests, and her mother stood behind the small counter, next to the opulent register. A selection of magazines was neatly arrayed on the glass top. When her mother raised one hand to fix an errant curl of hair, it was almost an occupation in itself, and her nails were perfectly enameled in pink; her hands looked fresh. She wore dresses now, some with a scooped neckline, and always a necklace of large white ceramic beads. A gift from Claude. Oddly, their daily take did not lessen, for Claude's hands and arms became a blur, and his routines and patter became famous. The Pittsburgh paper did a feature piece on him. Once, home during a break in a concert tour, Anne had come out to the airport to take them to dinner, and she stood in the obscurity of the hallway to admire Claude's act. Nor was she his only audience, because others on their way to their departure gates had also paused to admire the way he tossed the brush from hand to hand without losing a stroke, the few steps of the soft shoe routine he performed as he finished, snapping the cloth like a magician summoning a final miracle. One or two even applauded, and her mother seemed to accept their applause as her due as well, for she smiled graciously, one hand going to her bare throat.

"That's right; that's good," Claude said, and the two of them looked at each other as if they shared much more than this cubed box of light smelling of shoe polish.

But Anne had been spotted. "So there's that little girl with her violin who never would play for us," the customer said. He was an old customer and had been looking at her, finally making the identification.

"That is the very lady," Claude said. "She's the toast of the Big Apple. She's playing for royalty these days. No way to hear her in this shoe shop." Claude circumspectly turned and guided the man toward the cash register while whisking the material of his suit. "Yes, that's right."

Her mother rang up the register and took the man's money. She folded and refolded the edge of her dress collar as she stood before the neat array of shoe polishes and looked out into the darkness to where Anne leaned against the wall. Their eyes seemed to meet, but her mother looked away still smiling and carefully lined up the magazines on the countertop.

Anne's agent was always happy to hear from her, breathlessly attentive, as if her office were being radically redecorated around her even as she talked. "I'm in Melbourne next February?" Anne asked. It had grown dark, and the airport lights had come on.

"Yes, that's right. February. Why?"

Anne watched a woman with two children hanging on her, stop, look around, then pick up a duffel bag and continue. "What's the matter?" the agent said quietly.

"I think I want to take a year off. I'm tired."

"Oh, really."

"I think I want to look at something else. Maybe the Tchaikovsky book."

"Tchaikovsky? You playing Tchaikovsky? What's all this about?"

"And I think I'll start wearing my hair differently, so we'll need new pictures."

"Look," her agent said after a moment. She probably had lit one of those small cigars she favored. "Look, call me after Denver, and we'll talk about this. Okay? That's what we'll do. But don't think about this until after Denver. Promise me? Anne, promise me?"

"Yes, I promise," she said, feeling like a schoolgirl, pleasantly guilty.

Her flight had been announced; boarding would commence in fifteen minutes. Time to get to a loo; she hated the cramped arrangements on planes. And she had the place to herself; all of its spotless impersonality made a kind of clearing in her head. On one wall, a fold-down shelf had been mounted on which diapers could be changed. She pulled it down and rested her violin case upon it, unfastened the clasps. This was her baby, and—she had understood for some time the only baby she would have, beautifully formed, responsive to her slightest caress and fitting so sweetly, so perfectly under her chin. She cradled the instrument in her left arm and took out the bow. There was no window in the bathroom, but one wall of glass brick, which gave a garbled view of the outside. She took up her stance and considered the possibilities. A phrase from Brahms perhaps, maybe a lullaby.

Mourning After

It was Mel's idea. When the lumberyard closed down, we had gone our separate ways with families and odd jobs. Living across town from each other, there'd been little chance to shoot some darts or to have a beer or two, which had been our pleasure after work. I'd heard his wife had died and his children were living in California. There's a loneliness that comes with retirement nobody mentions in the benefits office, and when a man stops working it's like he gives up a part of his citizenship. So when the phone rings one morning, and Mel starts talking, the years between magically disappeared. He could have been calling about some new prefab unit the boss had ordered.

"I suppose you saw the announcement of Jed Baker's passing," he starts right off without a hello or how-are-you. That was his way. I tell him the sports pages were my interest, not the obituaries. "They've got him down at the Swanson Family Home, and tonight's the layout. I thought you might like to join me to pay respects to our fallen colleague."

Now I never liked Jed Baker. He ran the account department like it was a branch of the Internal Revenue Service, and he never had an agreeable word for anyone. Sour would be a fair description. We'd have contractors waiting for their orders, on their knees practically and threatening to go elsewhere, and Baker would be taking his sweet time in that inner office, filling in all the lines, crossing the T's a certain way. But it had been years since Mel and I had got together, so it seemed a good chance to catch up.

"Where you going?" the wife asks after supper. I had cleaned up a little, so she had spotted something was afoot.

"Old Jed Baker died, and some of us from the yard are paying our respects. He's down at the Swanson Family Home." Her eyes become pieces of shale that catch me in their gleam.

She still holds that business with Rosie up to me, though that was way back and Rosie long gone. I admit lately to have thought about that woman and how her chestnut curls would come undone when we played bandits at the Full Moon Motel on Route 24. Someone told me she had gone blond just before the end in Cincinnati.

I have no trouble recognizing Mel. He's sitting on the first landing of the high steps that go up to the funeral home, long legs crossed more than once it seems, and his back straight as a ruler. He's smoking, and his neck and some of his chest come naked and red from the open collar of a green sport shirt. That was Mel all right, not about to dress for anyone's ceremony. His hair is now pure white but still thick and combed flat to his head and over his ears, like it's been sprayed on.

"Those Camels are going to get you—don't you read the papers?" I say by way of greeting.

"Hey there, old timer." He stands up and takes my hand. "Didn't this house used to belong to that guy who went to prison?"

"The honorable James T. Walsh," I reply. "He embezzled city funds to pay for his sweetie's swimming pool." I look up at the huge front porch of the mansion at the top of the terrace. The porch sweeps around to one whole side of the building where I can see part of the steep roof of another building that must have been a carriage house. Groups of people stand on the porch talking. Some carpenter must have had a fine time with all the finials hanging from that roofline.

"They lived well, didn't they?" Mel says and takes my arm as we climb the stone steps.

We had never met any of Baker's family; the man kept to himself and more or less lined up with management, though he was far from that. But his survivors are an attractive-looking bunch and earnest in their grief. The widow is plump and bright eyed. You can tell she might have been pretty at one time. "Thank you so much for coming," she says, shaking my hand. The warmth in her greeting moves me, so I am glad we have shown up, and I may have stretched my response more than I had contemplated.

"He was a fine man," I tell her. "Everybody liked and respected him because he was such a hard worker." No sense being truthful at a time like this.

Next to me, I hear Mel telling one of the sons that his father had been an "integral and important member of our community," which wasn't Mel's usual language, so I figure he must have read it somewhere.

Funeral homes don't bother me much except for that sickly perfume that's supposed to add to the flowers that are always in numbers. Some places lay it on so thick you suspect the undertaker wasn't all that confident about his own craft, a more objectionable smell might be about to take over. Also, since Bobby's funeral, it's like I've been immunized to the whole show.

Mel has made a beeline for the open casket set up at the far end of an inner room. Flowers are everywhere, which makes you wonder that Baker must have had friends unaccounted for at the lumberyard. The peachy-colored light seems to give off the smell of the fruit itself. We take up a respectful manner, shoulder to shoulder, and look down at the deceased.

"Time took its toll with old Jed," Mel says after a while. "But he still kept some of his hair."

I study the face in the casket, and it is true—the years have made quite a difference in the man. "Mel," I finally say, "Jed Baker was as bald as a chicken egg."

"That has puzzled me too," he says softly. Neither of us has made a move, not a tremor to give away our wonder. "Perhaps it's an example of the funeral director's art," Mel offers. Mind you, all of our discussion is low key—just above a murmur—and we must resemble a pair of old guys going over the good times with the deceased. I can almost feel other people taking us in like we are special witnesses to this unfairness of life. "But then there's the nose," Mel has continued. "Check out the nose."

"Like a button," I say.

"Right," Mel says. "Not the sharp dagger that son of a bitch used to stick into your expense account every month."

"Son of a bitch," I agree.

"You know something, old timer." Mel looks up with a merry eye. "We're at the wrong funeral. My eyes are not what they used to be. I read Swanson, but he's probably down at the Swenson place on Wyandotte Boulevard. They use that tiny print for the obituaries."

"You've nailed it," I whisper.

So we have this embarrassment and stand there like a couple of boys caught with our hands in the cookie jar—though there's probably a better way to say that. How are we going to turn around and get out without encountering questions we can't answer? It would be crude to partake of the drink and "funeral meats," as the poet describes them, that are sure to be offered in some adjunct premise, but to leave without tasting anything would seem both cold and cruel. Mel has the solution. He whips out his handkerchief and covers his whole face like someone caught in a sandstorm and heads for the exit. I follow quickly behind him, my hand on his shoulder, both to support and guide him in his overwhelming woe.

"That was quite a performance," I tell him as we have a beer in a nearby tavern. "They must have thought he owed you a ton of money. Debt canceled by death."

"I'm not a bit sorry about the mistake," Mel says after his laughter dries up. "Think of that family hearing so much praise from two complete strangers. Must have made them feel the old fart was an outstanding citizen."

"We could still get down to the other place," I suggest. "Make it a double header."

"Naw, what the hell." Mel shrugs and pulls one foot up on the seat of the booth, his knee under his chin like the basketball star he might have been if he'd stayed in school. "The important thing is that we got together—you and me. That's the real outcome of it."

That was characteristic of him all over, making a positive consequence out of something that had gone flat. How many times over the years did I watch him, standing next to me at the counter, talking to some contractor or private citizen about the plywood or the tile they had ordered that had been put on indefinite hold and then coming up with a different item, an alternative we had in stock? And how many times did I see those same clients come back to thank him because the substitute had worked better than the original choice?

You don't find that happening today. You can stand in some of these places for twenty-four hours only to encounter a salesperson who always seems to be running the other way with a full bladder. And it's a little scary to be all alone and surrounded by bins of silent lumber stacked in multitudes, and fastenings of all sorts, and not a single other human in sight. It's like you've landed in purgatory.

Mel orders another round from this mean-looking waitress. "I expect there are bereaved families all over town, as we take our leisure, that would be both amazed and appreciative if a couple of gents like us showed up to heap praise on their sorrowful loss." He sips the foam of the new lager, and he looks as if he's found it particularly refreshing. But the idea has just hit.

"You know what we ought to do," he says finally. "We ought to appoint ourselves a two-man delegation of sympathy. Think of the poor bastards that don't have anyone to speak well of them at times like this. How do you suppose their families feel—their children suffering anonymity and disgrace? We could drop by the viewing and pass a few words that would brighten the family history and lighten the mournful load. Moreover, there's sometimes good eats."

So, it is another example of how great ideas are born in the simplest of surroundings. We began attending funerals all over town to comfort the bereaved and pay our respects, and we were always welcomed. Mel picked the event, and he'd read the obituaries with considerable care. "There's an interesting case down at the Ciueslak Home," he'd say on the phone. "A forty-year man at the foundry works, and a veteran too." Or he'd start talking without a hello. "Here's one that just cries out for our attention. Fella worked for the gas company and retired twenty years back. But listen to this—he seems to be survived only by an unmarried daughter. They got him at the Rose of Sharon Chapel."

After several run-throughs, we got our act together pretty good. Solemnly, we'd take our place in line and then put a meaningful grip on the hand of a family member, look them right in the eye, and say how the likes of the deceased would never be seen again. So, you could say there was always some truth in our pronouncements. Nor did we always work in tandem. Sometimes, I'd wait outside as Mel ran the gauntlet, then I'd come in and work the line, all of which gave a breadth to the communal sorrow, that more than one neighborhood was bereft.

After each layout, we'd review the event in a local bar, going over how the different family members had reacted, the measure of their gratitude, and the marks of their surprise. "I never knew Dad had so many friends," a woman tells us.

"He was modest about his friendships," Mel confides softly.

"But always there when you needed him," I add. She looks like she was about to laugh but then sobs into her hanky.

Amazement and wonder, gratitude and appreciation—we encountered every expression imaginable. It cheered me to think we were bringing to these survivors knowledge about the departed they had never suspected—examples of generosity and endeavor that totally surprised them but that would warm the cup of memory for the rest of their days. Now and then, in our effort to introduce an interesting angle on the man, we would go too far in our reminiscence.

"My husband never fished a day in his life," this widow tells us one night. She's keeping the vigil all by herself, no other family members present, and I guess Mel was prompted to overcompensate because of the small turnout.

I can almost hear the gears shifting behind his eyes. "No question you're right," he says after pulling his tongue out of his throat. "But this one time took place during our lunch break. You remember," he turns to me for confirmation, "how old George went down to the river and hung that line off of one of the barges and pulled in that black bass?"

"Just like that," I affirm and nod at the woman.

"Must have been at least a ten pounder," Mel continues.

"Oh, I'd say fifteen if it was an ounce." She's looking back and forth between us like we are a tennis match. I go on, "He slapped that sucker down on a sheet of chrome that had just rolled out of the furnace and grilled it to perfection." Mel blinks a couple of times, and I could see he has nowhere to go.

"Tasty eating," he finally says.

"He never told me about any of that," the widow says with a tight smile. She looks around the near empty room for something she might have misplaced.

"The man always had a modesty about him," Mel says and leads the way to the bier. "Can you see any wildness or originality in that face? Any check in the grain?"

"None whatsoever," I agree. "But she's going to remember that fish story for sure. Something she can take out and enjoy on a quiet evening."

Right then, the funeral director approaches us, and you can see his face shaping a few questions. But I compliment him on his presentation, and that sidetracks him, because, like the rest of us, these fellows like to have their work appreciated.

Mel and I came to know the ins and outs of many of the city's establishments—like wine connoisseurs you might say. How the casket was placed, the flower arrangements, the lighting, and the general appearance of the remains—we'd go over these points after each occasion. Of course, the funeral homes began to know us too, and a couple of the owners made sly remarks about us having a wide circle of friends, all of them kicking off within spitting distance of each other. But there were no complaints—I mean we didn't steal anything—and being part showmen themselves, these funeral directors may have appreciated us taking part to "swell the scene," as the poet has written.

"Where you off to tonight?" the wife would ask. That wrongdoing of nine years back still makes her suspicious.

"I'm meeting up with Mel," I'd say. "Shoot some darts."

"Last time you came back, you smelled like a smokehouse."

"He's still puffing," I answer. She looks me over with all the leaden regard of someone who has bought something that can't be returned. I know what she's thinking.

Rosie smoked in that careless way, holding the cigarette in the same hand she ran through her hair as she talked, slow and thoughtful. Then, her hair falling over my nakedness would transfer the smell of the tobacco on to me.

It's a sad aspect of life that love and living with someone doesn't always go together. I mean, I love my wife, but living with her is almost pure hell, and I expect she feels the same way. Then there's lust to make the third leg of this stool we're given to sit on. That was Rosie. One evening as we were preparing to part, I was feeling a little down, and I must have looked it. "Look here," Rosie said sharply, "we mustn't let this lust we have seep into love!"

Before Bobby took sick he told me about a book he was reading at school wherein some philosopher gave the opinion that humans were originally all one being. But then some ancient god, looking for sport, divided us into men and women, and we've been trying to get back together ever since. But it makes you wonder why the god we worship these days didn't put us back together instead of leaving things how he found them.

So the love that was between the wife and me only made the disagreements all the more painful, whether they were about a TV show or when to put out the garbage. If we could have lived apart, I think the love we had would have taken over, been expressed, and Rosie probably would not have happened. But she did show up, one Monday in bookkeeping with that mass of curls and a laugh that knew all the answers and none of them funny. She had the same problem with her husband, a trucker.

All that one spring and part of the summer, we kept our lust contained until someone in bookkeeping—one of those old biddies I imagine—tipped Rosie's husband, and he pulled up stakes and moved his trucking business downstate. It was a smooth operation, done several times before, I imagine, and with no complaints from Rosie. I don't remember how she said good-bye. The wife must have got the information from the same source, and I was sorry about the whole business.

Mel's cough is getting worse, and it takes him a while on the phone to get organized this last time. Finally, he is able to talk. "We got a hot one tonight. The guy was a foreman down at the freight depot and a VFW post commander. Also a big shot with the Knights of Columbus. This could be an ultimate occasion."

"We've never done anyone this close to management before," I say.

"Don't be a snob," he replies. "Death is the great equalizer." He continues to pull himself together. "It promises to be a big blowout and a test of our abilities. Also, it's at the O'Connor Home, and they always do a tasteful job of it. I remember your appreciating their musical selections."

Now it has begun to occur to me that in mollifying the grief of others we might be addressing our own sadness. When we make up these stories about the deceased, the compliments and all, we are also making ourselves up. And getting dressed for the wake—wasn't I feeling the same as I did those times when I got ready to meet Rosie? The guy in the mirror knotting his tie is the same guy I see there every day, but he is thinking he's about to become special—unique. Like there are two mirrors but just one of me to look at.

"So where are you off to tonight?" the wife asks. She has settled down before the TV, the program schedule in one hand, ready for the evening to unfurl.

"Just another frolic with old Mel," I reply, but I'm not laughing. Something heavy has fallen all the way down to the bottom of me as I view the back of her head bent forward a little from the recliner. She has just chosen a quiz show.

So, I'm on the sidewalk outside the O'Connor place, waiting for Mel. He was right; the layout is well attended, and the mourners have a satisfied look about them, as if they've just got up from a fine dinner. The music from inside seems to keep time with how they climb the steps, like in one of those old-time newsreels, but I can tell by looking that none has anything more interesting to say about the deceased than I do, and they've known the guy. So, it isn't that I feel out of place. Just then, Mel comes into view, and I'm surprised to see him wearing plain pants and a heavy sweater with his shirt collar open. Stickler for details, he has dressed to represent the workforce the guy inside had supervised. In a respectful sort of way, he tosses his cigarette into the gutter and takes the steps up to the porch.

"You've been in already?" he asks. He looks a little worried.

"No, I was waiting for you." He takes my arm and makes a start for the door, but I stay put. The music inside sounds like tiny crystal leaves falling. He's been looking in my face, waiting for some explanation. Finally I say, "Just not my night, I guess."

He smoothes the hair back around his ears and looks away, and then he nods. His arms fall to his sides. "Sure, I can understand. We all have those. Well, I guess I can get it done by myself." He squares his shoulders like some actor in the movies and smiles, but there is no real fun in it.

"I'm sorry," I say and really mean it.

"I'll be in touch," he says as I start down the steps.

"You're home early," the wife says. One of those programs that have experts giving value to antiques is on.

"Mel didn't show up." It's not the first time I've lied to her.

"I think the pie is still warm in the oven," she says.

Solitaire

Dad is here, I say, and then you answer something like—Oh, I'm so happy you are having this time together with your father—though just a minute before you were saying you had this big problem you hoped I could take care of, thinking your words were daring, dirty-boy talk that went along with clapping erasers together in the seventh grade outside of Horace Mann in Blue Springs—Hey, Emily, we got problems with our homework. Give us a hand?

"What's that, Dad?"

He is saying that he has to use the last four digits of his Social Security number as a code to get into this new condo he's moved to from Blue Springs. He is sitting at the kitchen table, playing solitaire, and I can see his neck has gotten thin; the cords strain into his skull like cables pulling up the rest of him, holding the rest of him up by his ears it seems like, because they have gotten much larger.

"It's a damn nuisance," he says and lays down a black seven neatly on top of a red eight.

"What's that, Dad?"

"Memorizing those damn numbers. You have to punch them into this panel by the mailboxes and then run across the foyer to the door and grab the handle while it's still buzzing."

"I guess it must be for your security, though," I say.

"I never had to remember all these numbers before," he says. "Never." He gets an ace free and puts it down above the others.

You'll have to get that cleaned off the table, Momma would say, I'm serving dinner in ten minutes. Hold your horses, he'd say, I almost got this worked out. Why don't you give me a hand, and I'll get done faster.

So you all talk like that no matter your age, whether it's playing cards or whatever. Just last week, this director of consumer relations leans across the crudités at this reception and tells me how he would like to pin things down, open them up and then pin them down. So I pass him the olives that have all these toothpicks sticking up in the air, and he looks at them for a second and then says, no thanks.

I must remind myself that I am a woman with a boy-child, like tonight, when I heard your voice on the phone, saying those dumb fuck things, and I'm going along with it—I reach up to my hair and expect to find rollers—and then I turn around, and there's Dad with his cards all laid out, and stuck on the fridge door is that card Billy gave me—"Happy Birthday to Mom, the Apple of My Eye."

Sometimes your eyes have a way of rolling up and you look like Our Savior on the cross, I mean the statues I used to pray to, look up to from my knees, and catch just a glimmer of whites as he bore his blessed agony. "Always surprised that you feminists went in for this sort of thing," you said the other afternoon before your eyes slipped back into your skull, though I expect your agony was not all that unbearable. All this talk shocks me a little, mixing all these subjects up together, but not the language so much as the mix of them.

"Playing those drums noon and night," Dad is saying. "They must be students from Africa who have rented the apartment below me. I've spoken to the people in the front office about it. But they're a whole new crew down there—bunch of young girls who don't care much about anything save fixing up their faces and going out to lunch. Meanwhile, it's boom-la, boom-la, boom-la—BOOM." The four of hearts cracks down and a whole run is precipitated. He might win this game.

"Did you talk to the students about the noise, Dad?"

"That does no good. They won't listen to me."

Is that true about ears getting bigger as you get older? Dad's ears seem to stick out a lot more than I remember. I think of one fall afternoon, tramping through the woods back of our house, trying to keep up with him, wanting to snuggle into his broad red-and-black plaid back against the autumn chill, his shoulders large and his neck just right and his ears neat—tucked into a Minnesota Vikings cap. He walked so fast.

You told me the ears keep growing. Too bad for you, you said, that the other parts stop, and I laughed so I wouldn't be embarrassed by the silly-ass purity of your remark—your humor sometimes wears black socks, if you know what I mean—or give you any idea I might have been offended. All these names you give things, all the parts called something, labeled. It's a nomenclature I find gratuitous, but the names don't bother me. They bother you, I think. You say them maybe just to bother yourself. The language is almost enough for you, which brings me back to the ears business. I was laughing, even threw a pillow at you if I remember rightly, so as to keep you busy while I had time for my own thoughts. If the ears get bigger, then we should hear better, we should listen to each other better. Better.

"It's terrible," Dad says. "You can't hear yourself think."

"I get the feeling," I say, "that you don't like your present situation."

And that stumps him. He has to think about that for a little. He pats the cards and puts them straight.

Let me get back to being shocked. It's not what you think. You might think I am having trouble keeping my different selves apart—the old naming of the parts again. But why is it you have to separate everything? I guess putting a tag on something is to claim it, but to identify is not to understand anything. One is subjective, comes from the imagination of the beholder, and the second is a given—the basic rose, you might say.

Last week, I glanced in the mirror on the way to the bathroom, and I saw Billy's mom, the apple of his eye, and just then you said my ass looked like a peach. I am an orchard, is that it? A one-tree orchard with all of you perched on different limbs, enjoying the different fruits, but just one tree? You understand? I don't think you do. Listen.

Tuesday I had gone to bed early to work on some reports and the door opens and here comes Billy to climb under the covers and lie against me, all five feet of him from toe to shoulder lined up against me. So I shift from vice president of the credit bureau to Mom and then I think of Billy's father—because that's why the boy is in bed with me, he's lonesome for his father and I'm only a substitute—then the phone rings and I know it's you calling. Remember, you were in a bar in Germantown? Want to come out and play? you were saying, like you had just discovered sandboxes, and you were cute, right enough, I admit to a little burn even with Billy lying close beside me and these market evaluations in my lap.

"There, Dad," I say. I reach over his shoulder and point to the nine of hearts.

"I see it," he says. "I was just looking for a better play."

But he hadn't seen it and he has no better play and his voice had that edge to it that Momma used to laugh at and turn back to the kitchen after she had wondered out loud if it wasn't a good idea to call a plumber about the leak and save Dad's good clothes for Sunday instead of him trying to patch it himself. And I agreed with his labeling of her just then, with the sound in his voice that said she didn't know what she was talking about—oh, I wish we could run history backward like a movie, so Momma would come backward out of the kitchen, turn around just after Dad had snapped at her, so I can say—Look here, Momma, he can't even spot the nine of hearts, can't see the card exposed right here under his nose. But the reason I said nothing then is the same reason I put up with your dumb shit talk—I was waiting right then for him to come out and push me in that swing he had rigged up in a big oak in the side yard. Oh, he would push me so high that I'd leave my breath up there in the leaves. You push me high like that sometimes, but I know better than to trust your expertise on plumbing. Do you follow me?

So we've made some gains, maybe—but it's still swing time, and I'm the tree. That story you told me the other night about that girl changing into a tree to escape Apollo, was it? You like those corny plots, old-time gods chasing girls into trees, and you recite them to me as if they have something to do with us. You almost get teary telling it. How romantic, how wonderfully sad it was that the gods felt sorry for the girl and changed her into a tree so as to escape Apollo—and it was a laurel tree—so all the heroes thereafter get to wear her leaves around their heads. But why did she have to become a tree at all? Why didn't Apollo leave her alone in the first place? Why didn't the gods change him into something—say, a rock or a stump?

• • •

Dad is here to help me move my furniture. The suite arrived on Friday. He doesn't so much move as to be a pivot as I move. Billy's away with his wilderness group, and don't be hurt I didn't call you to give me a hand—believe me, I thought of it—but Dad needs some activity, some rolling up of the sleeves to look things over. What do you call that? he said yesterday. That's a lamp, I said. But before that, he kept on. Well, I guess it was one of those Russian samovars, I replied. To make tea in. And he stepped back a little to squint at it.

It's the most he can do these days—that stepping back for one more incredulous look—to evaluate my peculiar way of doing something. He took the divorce harder than I or even Billy has. Because when I divorced David, I deprived Dad of a companion in disbelief, a fellowship in shirt-sleeves—the two of them turning to each other and saying, Just what the hell is she up to now? United Chums and I'm something from a Third World to shake their heads over. What's the offer? Sovereignty? Is that it? My own flag and certain trade rights?

"Boom-la!" Dad says. He's just uncovered the king of hearts that he's needed for several hands. Now he shifts the queen of clubs over and uncovers the ace of diamonds. The last bullet.

"You're going to win it, Dad."

Tell me the truth—I'm losing you, aren't I? I can smell good-bye on you like rain coming. You're telling me right now about your week's sched-ule; you're telling me about this problem you have right now—but all by telephone. You used to appear on my doorstep with your problems, like the paperboy. In fact, you bear some resemblance to the paperboy, or maybe I think of you bringing me bad news along with the good. I'm always saying or doing things that shock you, and I guess that's some of my appeal, because you feel free to do and say stuff you always wanted to say and do back in the seventh grade, and it tickles you that I know all the words and that it's okay to say them to someone who looks like me, a mom and a vice president.

But it's the words beyond those you hear me use—and that bothers all of you—that would make it all come out right, card for card. Maybe I don't like my situation either, and I have a whole bunch of numbers to memorize just to get through doors that ought to be open to me around the clock—but that's the way you do things—for my security, you say, but it isn't really for my security but maybe yours. Just to walk through the same door with you is not the limit of my aspiration. But, I prefer it to being given my own door on the other side of the building. Sovereignty is no guarantee of equality.

"It's not the same thing," I tell Dad. I just caught him shuffling the last of his cards. "You have to play them as they come out, how they were dealt.

He needs one card to clear the board, win the game, and it's the ten of hearts and it's stuck in the pack. He can see it and he has tried to shuffle the cards so it comes out on top. I've ruined it for him, handed back to him the rules of solitaire he taught me, and I can see he's a little angry to be caught out.

"Damn it, look at that," he says. He's gone through the same set of cards several times, and the red ten stays in the same place—one card from the top, one card away from freeing up the rest of them.

"I'm sorry, Dad," I say as you're saying these things to me across the wire that stretches taut from the wall when I lean across his shoulder. You offer tenderloin black and blue. A bottle of '05 Bordeaux. And this problem of yours that is getting bigger by the minute. Yes, I am tempted. But I'm tantalized by something else, which is what I've been trying to say to you all along.

"Do it again, Dad. Try a new game." He's been grimly obeying the rule I've reminded him of, that I've held him to. The ten of hearts refuses to move up in the pack, stays where it can be seen but never played. It never gets clear between us either, even though we keep turning the cards over and over and you think these highs you push me to are the solution—that I like them so much it somehow puts us on the same level, or I'll go along with the rest of it. Like I'm on your side.

But as the lady said, *I find this frenzy insufficient reason for conversation when next we meet.* Can you imagine someone like Edna St. Vincent Millay being changed into a tree? Not on your tintype, nor me either, lover. But at the same time, I see something that's never played out if we go by the rules. I keep seeing it just under the top card—always there and teasing me to keep turning the same cards over, time and again, hoping this game will come out right, so I'm more than willing to play with you, thinking one time that red ten will come free—will set us both free.

But not tonight. And I don't know when either. Maybe never. You don't like to hear that. You say you love me, but that scares me a little. A lady can change her mind. That's one of those rules the United Chums have passed for the benefit of us in the Third World to make us feel equal. It comes with our domain—we're allowed to change our minds. Close up the show. Changing our minds is expected of us. Like some of the natives being slow in the sun.

"Those are the rules you taught me, Dad," I say. He mumbles something under his breath, then slowly scoops up the cards, starts to shuffle the whole deck together. He was only about two or three cards from winning. I'm hanging up now. Enjoy your steak and the Haut-Medoc. I'm getting the other deck of cards out and we'll see how we do doubled up. Maybe it will come out right. Thanks for calling.

The Italian Grammar

Only Nick Jones may have looked on Eva Landers bare, though some of us claimed the vision during those bull sessions in the Eisenhower era. "Shameful, all that talk," Eunice says the other morning, lips pursed above her teacup. Lately, we've switched to herbal teas, but dreams yet rummage my sleep. "Things," she continues, underscoring the noun, "have been set just a bit right since that obnoxious time." She looks me in the eye as if I were about to object to the advances women have made, their new opportunities and the rest of it. "I wonder if she still has that Italian grammar I loaned her," Eunice adds and turns round to check the toast. If she were not a librarian, would she feel this way about this overdue book?

For this is not the first time Eunice has brought up that grammar Eva borrowed almost thirty years ago. No, to be more precise, Eunice *loaned* the book and then only because of that chance encounter in the Village. What was the name of that place? Something like Da Stephano, and we had just moved into this apartment. One balmy fall Sunday, we walked over to the Village and passed the window of this small restaurant, set down a few steps under a brownstone. Red-checked tablecloths and bread sticks in a tumbler on each table; it had all the trite appeal of the time—determined naïveté flung over the commonplace.

"Well, hello." Eva stood above us at our table. She held a pencil and note pad in a thoroughly professional manner, though something was amiss, as there always was with Eva—a shift sidewise of those remarkable violet eyes as if on the lookout for adults who might expose her charade. We hadn't seen each other in a half dozen years, the whole bunch of us—with the exception of Eunice—all together in Cambridge. Eva's liquid gaze had just dissolved that chunk of time. She leaned forward and carefully lit, after several failed matches, the candle stuck into the Chianti bottle.

"She has money?" Eunice observed more than inquired as Eva disappeared behind the swinging kitchen door to get our antipasti. "She doesn't need to work here."

"Some, maybe," I replied. As a matter of fact, the great variety of cashmere sweaters Eva had always worn hinted at money—soft turtlenecks in dark colors that lushly implied the sumptuous breasts within. On the other hand, most of us at Harvard then were there thanks to the GI Bill, so any apparel distinctive from the military castoffs we pulled on every morning was certain to seem luxurious.

"I want to go to Italy next year," she told us, putting down the scaloppine. "I took this job to learn Italian." Eunice looked at me hard, and I changed the subject.

"Heard from any of the others?" I asked. "I saw a poem of Jesse Warner's in *The Nation* awhile back. And I ran into Andy at Chumley's. He's up for a part at the Cherry Lane. An O'Neill play the Clancy brothers are doing. He's changed his name to Cole. Have you seen Nick Jones?"

Eva pulled a strand of coal black hair across her face, and her purplish eyes had gone vague. A visor had come down. "He's around I guess."

This dialogue was making Eunice impatient; after all, it wasn't her "old gang," and she had turned on her veal with a deft precision. Yet, as always, her generous nature eventually rose to embrace the moment. "I have a very fine Italian grammar I would be happy to lend you. It might offer a wider vocabulary than these menus can provide."

I think Eunice may have been surprised when Eva accepted, but we exchanged phone numbers, and so this random event had happened. Lately, suspicions have arisen as to the part chance plays in history—that it is equal to any other determination, and those who survive, who become important, are merely only luckier than those who do not. The success of a species, of an individual, may have less to do with selection according to fitness than with where one is standing in the savanna when the sky falls. The great rocks that squashed reptilian sovereignty could drop again to stamp out Shakespeare, Homer, Chartes, and Yankee Stadium. All pure chance.

"Bad dreams again, darling," Eunice said the next morning. She looked pink and eager to get up to Forty-second Street. That's how we met. I needed some dates for my dissertation and had gone into the reference room of the public library, and this very pretty young woman helped me out. So very efficient, capable, and her assurance impressed me even more. She not only knew what she was doing, but seemed very confident she should be doing it. She had found her place already with an almost feudal satisfaction. Her self-confidence was not only appealing but curiously erotic. I invited her out for some Chinese that same evening.

"Meeting Eva has made me think of Nick Jones," I told her, but she wasn't prepared to listen. The vast solitude of the library was calling to her, her own enclave within that immense privacy. Actually I had not only been thinking of Eva Landers but wondering how I might pass the Italian grammar on to her. Eunice had left the book on the sill of our kitchen window that looks down on Avenue C.

• • •

So, running into Eva at Da Stephano had also called up Nick Jones, as unwelcome a ghost at that modest meal as he was in those days when we resented him sitting down at our high table. Those of us who had only recently faced death or had done others to death resented his cocky manner, his offhand handling of the war that had interrupted and qualified our lives. We didn't hold against him he had spent the war writing speeches for generals in public relations. The luck of his draw. Chance again. But it was his jaunty manner that seemed to claim more; even the boots he wore in winter bothered us, for they gave off the cavalier style of an ex-flyboy, whereas it was the studious, shy Jesse Warner who had flown thirty missions over Germany. So, Nick, maybe without intending to do so—to give him some credit—seemed to present something he was not. He was attractive, a bit of a show-off, and, in our opinion, not very deep.

Eva's voice on the phone sounded small and childlike, reminding me of how she and a couple of her girlfriends had this passion for *Winnie-the-Pooh*. They talked to each other in *Milnese*, if you will, and this childish whimsy mixed with their mature sensuality made a perverse potion that ravished us ex-GI's. Well, as a matter of fact, she told me on the phone, she was just going out, to the Metropolitan Museum. Why didn't we meet there? She wanted to see an exhibit of Christopher Wren's later sketches, because she had been auditing some lectures on architecture at the New School.

So we began to meet. I never told Eunice of these meetings. They went on for a year, but she would have gotten the wrong idea. Nothing happened, I mean. On the other hand, what was the right idea?

• • •

Retirement from the classroom has not come easy for me. Others may hurrah their syllabi into the air, but the classroom was my cosmos, a luminous sphere from within which I viewed the turns of the planet. Time for my real work now, Eunice says, but the proofs of my new book lie unexamined on my desk. My account of the Paris Commune has lost its urgency; those barricades seem puny obstacles to the events rushing down the avenues of CNN. At the same time, I've caught up on my reading, outside the discipline, which ironically has been partly supplied by this very same Nick Jones. His most recent novel is on the sideboard of our living room.

I must have all of his books, as he has sent them to me over the years, and I have watched his picture on the covers go from crisp studio poses to the fuzzy, almost amateurish image that takes up the whole back cover of the new book. It would be difficult to miss his splendid trajectory. Generous reviews in the *NY Times* from the beginning, and the latest making the front page of the *Book Review* with a copious second opinion in the *New York Review of Books* by Elizabeth Hardwick. Actually, his publisher sends me the books. Clearly, I'm on a list of some sort, and they arrive regularly like mail-order catalogs, uninscribed and unasked for. "With the compliments of the author," a card says, but I have to wonder about the compliment.

Because Nick Jones has certainly gone far beyond what any of us had expected of him. Our money was on people like Jesse Warner or Abe Rosen, who has had, in fact, some little success with that English-language newspaper he runs in Vienna, whether with the help of the CIA or not. Or to put my own two cents into the pot, my work (inclusion in *American Historians* and all the rest) has not let the old gang down either. I've often said that if we had come along in the '60s, some of us would be dead and the rest in prison, because if that little mimeographed broadsheet we put out didn't come close to sedition, it certainly kept us under the concerned scrutiny of the dean's office.

So, one day, this pup, with his overready smile and eager swagger, swung into our revolutionary cell by mistake. Did we know where the soccer club met? He had taken a wrong turn in the student union. Eva and her girl pals were kneeling on the floor, I remember, assembling and stapling the latest issue, and right off he began to tease them, calling them "handmaidens" in such a way as to get them laughing and blushing, especially Eva. As Abe Rosen liked to say, his intuition ran far ahead of his knowledge, and his prose was heavy with Hemingway.

So this morning, Eunice tells me this literary lion is to be celebrated at a special ceremony at the library to which, as curator of the Devlin Collection, she's been invited. Spouses are also welcome. "It will be a spiffy do," she tells me. "I'd think you'd be happy to witness your old chum being raised into the pantheon. Do you think he'll remember you?"

"Remember me?" I have to laugh. "He sends me all his books."

"Well, I'm off. I'm meeting Susan for lunch, and we're taking Master Matthew to Lord and Taylor for a new cap." She gives me a quick peck and is out the door. As she does with everything, Eunice has accepted her role as a grandmother as if it were something that came with her particular guild. Historical forces, objective or not, have never been a part of her philosophy.

Which brings me back to chance, the random sampling that puts one on the ladder above or below another. Nick Jones walking into our magazine's office that day, supposedly looking for the soccer team, but finding our project more interesting. "Well, it was Eva, old sport," he told me once. "Who wouldn't want to join up with an organization with a girl like that in its membership?" I'm pretty certain he had never read any Fitzgerald at that point, so his Gatsby lingo was just one more natural mannerism that annoyed us. He had not read anything in fact—not even Hemingway.

However, different volumes began to show up alongside the usual texts wedged under his left arm. Camus's *The Stranger*. Rilke's *Letters*. A slim collection of Primo Levi stories. "I don't get this guy Henry Green," I remember him telling us one afternoon. We were having coffee at the union. The next week, *Sons and Lovers* poked out of his raincoat. And so forth.

One evening, he rounded up and pushed some of us down to a storefront theater in Somerville for a production of Sarte's *The Flies,* in which Eva played one of the Furies. The place had been a small grocery and still smelled of root vegetables and cold cuts. The play's cast, in costume, served lemonade and raisin bran cookies at intermission. Eva looked not so much vengeful as a little dissolute, a Fury a bit hungover from the ongoing bash on Mt. Olympus. Her hands trembled as she handed up paper cups of lemonade, and I caught Jesse taking her in as she poured the stuff. The black leotard of her costume left little to the imagination. Then, Jesse looked at me and pulled my eyes over to where Nick gaily chatted up the other two Furies, Eva's girlfriends. A quick illumination shot between Warner and me: Eva had become Jones's cicerone through the inner circles of literature.

"How's your soccer game?" I remember Corky Roberts asked him one afternoon. We had settled into our usual large booth at the co-op, feeling a little high, for we had just published another issue of our thunderous gazette, and we were gleefully awaiting the sounds of outrage and dismay it was sure to cause the administration. In fact, I think Nick had a short piece in that issue, a harmless sort of memoir about his grandfather in Oklahoma, which a couple of us had to go over to bring up to snuff.

"Well, old sport," he replied to Roberts, "you fellows have given me a valuable insight—athletes may come and go, but a writer will always get the girl."

Just at the moment, as if summoned and looking a little dazed by the process, Eva appeared. "Ah," said Nick. *"Ecco proofo."* Eva blushed and looked sidewise.

"Hello, good-bye." She flicked some fingers and smiled. "I have to go. The magazine's been distributed. I have class."

These abrupt appearances and disappearances were part of Eva's fascination. In the same way, her concentration played a kind of hopscotch with a topic or an activity, and this was her manner when we met that first time in the Metropolitan. She started talking to me halfway across the huge foyer, where I had been waiting for her. "Oh, hello, here you are. Should we see the Egyptian first? The Wren is on the mezzanine. That new Bruegel is supposed to be worth a look. How nice, thank you." She took the Italian grammar. "Very kind of Eunice." She had slipped the book into her shoulder bag, and I was pretty sure Eunice would never see it again.

We saw the Wren and then the Bruegel; generally toured the Egyptian wing; not talking too much, not always viewing an exhibit together, but meeting often enough before a single painting so that people who saw us might have thought us a couple. We were to meet like that through the next four seasons—all innocent occasions and, actually, something Eunice had started by loaning her the grammar.

It was all in my head, but my disloyalty was especially evident after a fumbling gesture on that first afternoon. We were about to leave the museum when Eva turned suddenly about. "I want another look at that burial chamber. How it's put together. Amazing workmanship, don't you think?" She ran back to the Egyptian wing and slipped through the narrow opening in the facade of the reconstructed tomb. I found her inside, her face close to the interior wall, studying the stone mortise. In the dim light of that stone chamber, the royal blue of her sleeveless blouse became purplish black to set off a translucent quality in her bare arms and throat. She turned to me, her eyes wide with excitement. "Wonderful."

What had I been thinking? Heavy lipped and dark eyed, her expression within the cowl of her black hair was ancient and knowing. Her mouth fell into a smile, and she took a deep breath that seemed to draw me to her. "Oh, Billy." She laughed and gently held me off. "Not now."

Not now? Did she mean not then, but later? Did she mean not there, in this old tomb, but some place more comfortable? Or *not now* while she was pursuing her architectural interests—that these different interests should be kept separate? I never resolved the ambiguity of those two words, and I became stuck in them as if in amber.

For the next year I would follow Eva through those marble halls, an odd courtier, neither rejected nor favored, but happy to accompany her survey of that enormous collection, satisfied to take my place a step behind her as she idled before a Boucher. "Those little shepherdesses are a little naughty, don't you think?" she would say.

If I had the time, we would sometimes have lunch around the Roman pool, and she would report her changing interests between bites of green salad. She was studying film at NYU. She had signed up for modern dance at Barnard—her various enrollments and studies done in quick time but no less intensely. Once or twice, by the water lilies, her eyes would flick over my shoulder, and I got the impression that someone we both knew had passed behind me. I almost turned around. Once, she excused herself just as we sat down, but took so long at the ladies' room that her *potage haricot* was cold by the time she returned.

"Sorry, that damn line was so long." The soup's temperature made no difference to her. "Usually, I go to Frank's before I meet you."

"Frank's?"

"Frank Campbell's. You know, the funeral parlor on Madison." She broke the crusty roll over the soup bowl, dusting her fingers prettily. She had begun to wear very dark red nail polish. "They have a spiffy loo. There's almost always a layout, so I just sign the visitor's register and use the john. No dessert?"

In those days, my hours were determined by the department chairman, and I usually had to hurry back to a large lecture class on modern European history. So, no time for dessert, especially after Eva had spent an inordinate amount of time studying some Dürer engravings, line by line. Often, she would rush into the museum just as I would have to leave, but the apologies gasped were so winningly regretful, near disasters barely escaped just to meet me, that I always forgave her. "You won't believe what happened!" these prologues usually began, her purplish eyes lifted to the gallery as if to search out another audience.

"Oh, pooh," she said this afternoon. "I'll just have to have the crème caramel all by myself."

But did she? Had another gallant shadowed our footsteps through that treasure house? Another courtier waiting to take his turn at her elbow, or even elsewhere? Perhaps, I had merely been the foreplay, the sponsor of an excitement that another would fully enjoy? *Not now*, I heard her in my head. In retrospect, I wondered if that moment in the tomb had kindled her desire, but the protocol of that proper era, rather than she, had pushed me away. If I had pressed on through my own timidity, what might have happened? Right then and there? My imagination screened numerous scenarios. *Not now*, she had said, and I had meekly obeyed, perhaps to leave her prey to any stranger who might have come upon her as she took in Rembrandt's *Jolly Burgher*. Not a stranger. She wasn't so careless. It would have been someone she knew and could trust.

As I lurched back to Hunter on the crosstown bus, all these thoughts tumbled in my head, and I almost got off to double back to see who might be taking my place at her side, sharing the crème caramel. But by the time the bus reached Madison, Eunice's voice from that morning had restored my equilibrium. "Any socks for the wash, William?"

In any event, that spring saw the end of it. "I'm sorry to break our date." Her voice curved inside my ear. "I'm leaving for Rome tomorrow, and I have some things to do."

"Rome?"

"Yes, Rome, Italy," she specified as if I might have thought Rome, New York. I pictured a dazed look in her eyes, the quizzical smile. "I'm really going. I think I have some kind of a job with a movie company there."

She was as vague about the job as her adieu was offhand. For nearly a year, we had shared these moments at the Metropolitan, and she sounded as if she were breaking a dentist appointment. The toothache had disappeared, had been taken care of, and suddenly angry, I almost asked her if

Nick Jones was going along. Or she with him? He didn't, of course, and we know now that a destiny awaited Eva on the via Veneto far more glittering than what the halls of the Metropolitan could offer.

"Isn't this your Eva Landers?" Eunice asked one morning a couple of years ago. We were plowing through the Sunday *Times,* and she held out the open magazine to me. The article was on Ettore Rienzo, and a couple of pictures showed him working on *La Tabacchina,* what was to be his last film. One whole page was given to a semiformal portrait of him, sitting somewhat stiffly in an armchair and looking straight into the camera. His lined, Roman countenance was illuminated by the fiery genius in his eyes, and he seemed ageless, neither young nor old, like a bust of Dante or one of the Medici. And standing close behind him, also looking directly into the camera was Eva, her arms draped lovingly around his shoulders . . . *his American wife and muse since she produced his early triumph, "La Borsetta," which overnight placed him into a trinity with Fellini and Antonioni.*

The picture was a portrait of serenity, gave off a happy intimacy firmly grounded in success. The two of them reminded me of those clay couples comfortably at ease on the tops of Etruscan tombs. Eva looked remarkably unchanged. Her dark hair fell straight to her shoulders, cut in the familiar bangs along her forehead, but her eyes were different. No hazy restlessness stopped by the camera's shutter, but an expression focused on its own self-confidence. Nor can I remember her wearing so much jewelry. Several oversized bracelets lolled on the slender wrists crossed over the maestro's chest, and a heavy necklace, almost certainly of solid gold, fell into the deep line between her breasts, which the cut of her dress exposed. I almost laughed aloud at the memory of the little pair of earrings I had given her that Christmas of our year together, gold-rinsed reproductions of Bastet, the Egyptian goddess of pleasure, that I had bought at the museum's gift shop. "Oh gee," I remember her saying, when she finally arrived. "Little pussy cats."

"Undoubtedly, she's fluent in Italian by now," Eunice observes and pours us more tea. "But I told you she came from money—producing his movies."

"It says only the first one," I correct her.

"Are you all right, William?" She has been studying me. "You look funny."

I am fine, I tell her, even better than she can know. I was thinking that I had shared this fascinating woman with one of the giants of cinema, and this somehow rinsed away the sour suspicions I may have had about Nick Jones. So now, no doubt a punishment for my hubris, I will be forced to share Jones's lionization by the literary establishment at the library. Eunice insists that I accompany her to this ceremony at the Tilden-Astor Library. Trim as ever, her elegant legs still sprung by a youthful grace, she is a lovely antithesis to the stereotypical librarian that she sometimes presents with a charming self-mockery. My presence at the ceremony would completely, and once and for all, dispel that image, she says. Moreover, she reminds me, the library holds a couple of my own works in its permanent collection, a biography of Louis Napoleon and my monograph on the Internationale, a rare publication sought out by collectors today, so I've been told. I have as much right to be part of the scene as Nick Jones, Eunice tells me.

My classmate Corky Roberts—he's just retired from *Sports Illustrated*—has amused me over the years with his irreverent stories about old baseball players, about his encounters with a Duke Snider or a Willie Mays at some function sponsored by the magazine. He used to say that these flashbacks into an athlete's past heroics also called up his own youthful enthusiasms and energies at the time when he saw these men play, revisiting that guileless hunger to make a mark when the blackboard seemed wonderfully blank and accessible. So, a similar feeling comes over me as I stand in the marbled Renaissance lobby of the Tilden-Astor, because scattered around that huge expanse, nibbling paté and sipping chardonnay or soda water, are authors who had inspired and challenged me, who had once nurtured my dreams. Most look a little tired, perhaps weary of such events that require their presence, a little sodden around the edges. A portly Norman Mailer stands within a circle of admirers like the elder Cato, snapping at the immoral fat of our century. A gray, distant Styron leans into a conversation between two women editors as if the subject of that conversation were impaired rather than his hearing. *The Long March* was, I think, my generation's *Red Badge of Courage*. In the center of the hall, Kurt Vonnegut moves morosely toward the buffet, perhaps anticipating that he may have to step forward to admit the authorship of this very entertainment.

It is a pantheon, as Eunice called it. And all to honor Nick Jones, I must remind myself—a gabby, gobbling anthology of the nation's literary heart and muscle. A sort of feeding frenzy roils within this exalted pool; editors and agents swirl in and around the stolid leviathans, nipping and swiping here and there, piloted by what seem to be schools of startlingly beautiful young women. Later, in more than one chamber of this nautilus called Manhattan, lithe ambition will surely jockey flabby eminence.

Eunice is standing at the foot of the grand staircase, speaking animatedly with a man sitting on a marbled tread who carefully swirls the wine in his glass as he hears her out. He resembles the historian David McCullough, and I turn away quickly as Eunice looks up and around in midsentence, obviously trying to locate me. I see Nick Jones just as he sees me, and he raises one hand and waves. He stands beneath a bust of some immortal, merrily engaged by two women.

A flash of déjà vu takes me back to that opening night of *The Flies* in Somerville, but in this instance, one of the "handmaidens," to recall his term, is Elizabeth Hardwick and the other is Joyce Carol Oates, the latter hugged by him with such hardy fellowship that her cool tolerance seems dangerously crimped. He makes a courtly obeisance to these chatelaines of our national culture and strides across the great hall toward me with the smile of a victorious St. George.

It is a longish distance across the lobby, and he has it to himself, uninterrupted, save for the hesitant approach of a young woman whom he waves away without looking. The attention of that luminous throng has swung upon him, like the spotlight that follows an actor across a stage to where I stand in my baggy corduroys and mismatched tie and shirt—a second banana. "There you are, old sport." His hand is straight out before him from several feet away. "I hoped you would turn up."

The handshake was but the preface to a bone-snapping bear hug, and he lightly accepts my congratulations, as he reaches out to take a plain soda from a passing tray. "Well, king for a day, eh? Here today and gunned down tomorrow. But the work is all, as Uncle Henry said. That's important—getting the work down. You've proved it yourself. I read that book of yours. Louis Napoleon and his kidney stones. Great stuff. Great."

I turn aside his compliment. "To be sure, processing the raw material is important. But James also said we mustn't be put off by 'puerile—'"

"'Puerile fantasies.'" Amazingly, he's picked up my reference. "You got it. I bet you're the only one in this room, Billy-boy, to remember that quote. Aside from me, of course." His wink is broad and charming. "Like the old days when I'd sit down at the co-op to listen to all you geniuses talk." His exuberance for the "old days" continues as I review his recent work, how it has become overwhelmed by process. More than one opinion has noted that Jones's affection for postmodern farragoes has disconnected him from the true ground of his Oklahoma boyhood.

It's also my opinion that the truly important American novelists pack their imaginations into a wilderness of nostalgia, looking for that "fragment of lost worlds," as Fitzgerald called it, that tells us what we are by what we were. Many lose their way, and this description of Gatsby comes to mind as I look at Nick. I cannot remember his being this big with solid shoulders and a wrestler's neck. His hair is still thick, speckled with gray. Eunice has joined us.

"Great to see you, doll." His hug lifts my wife onto her toes. Normally, such an appellation would provoke a short, snappy lecture on objectification, but Eunice seems cheerful. "And I hear you're a big honcho upstairs. Smart and sexy. A winner."

"Really just a matter of attrition," Eunice says modestly. She has turned crimson, though her eyes send another message—that her position was not entirely due to a wearing down of antecedents.

I've just noticed that we have the alcove of this vast foyer to ourselves. No one comes near us, as if some tacit understanding has run through the assembly that we are to have this audience with Jones by ourselves. Perhaps, some have guessed that I am a long-lost brother, a quiet fellow who has just shown up from Hackensack, New Jersey. "William would know," I hear Eunice say as she turns to me. "You've heard from Corky just lately, haven't you?"

"He's moved to Coral Gables," I answer. "He just retired from *Sports Illustrated*."

"Flown south, eh?" Jones nods agreeably. "But he did okay. Managing editor or something like that, wasn't he?"

"Jesse Warner has a new book of poems out." I join his game of catch-up. "From the University of Arizona Press."

"Jesse Warner." He tries to put a face with the name and shrugs.

"A little shy," I fill in Jesse's blank a little. "He was our poetry editor, and most of the poetry we printed was his." We all laugh at that. "His new book is getting some good reviews. I just read one this morning," I tell Eunice. "In the *Kenyon Review*."

"Sorry, old sport. The mind is going." He winks at Eunice.

"Then, there's Abe Rosen."

"Oh yeah, Rosen, that CIA flack!"

"I'm not so sure there's any truth to those rumors."

Eunice has almost stepped between us, one hand touching the necklace around her throat. Pearls I gave her. "And Eva Landers? Her husband just died, didn't he? Rienzo?"

"Oh, dear Eva," Jones says and sips his soda. "One fascinating lady. I've been trying to put her into a book for years."

"You got to know her pretty well, I guess." My remark has pulled a serious look over his face. People have leaned over the balustrade above, looking down on the scene.

"Oh, we just horsed around. Just pals, really. I could never get through that A. A. Milne perimeter she put up around herself. You remember how she was." I shrug and look at Eunice. She looks pink with happiness, a fan's coloring. "Funny thing," Jones continues, "a few years after we graduated—I just got the Guggenheim, I think—I ran into her one afternoon at the Metropolitan."

"The museum?" I hear myself ask.

"Yeah, that one," Jones says and looks me over. Then he laughs. "Seems she hung out there, and I got the idea that she was meeting someone there. A ren-dez-vous as we Okies used to say. On the sly, if you get me." His wink was even broader but still directed toward Eunice, who giggled.

My voice seems trapped beneath my esophagus, fighting for expression and air in the clatter and din around us. "In fact," I finally manage to get out, "I did meet her at the museum. Once."

"Yes, William delivered a book I loaned her," Eunice says. "An Italian grammar."

"That one time. It was in the fall, as I remember," I say. That Eunice has made herself an accomplice to her own deception hits me hard.

"No, this was later in the year," Jones said. "Late spring. Daffodils up and the rest. She and the guy had this thing going on for some time. That was my impression. But you know how she could be." He's paused to look me over again. "She kept the different parts of her life put away in little boxes. Like handkerchiefs."

"A fascinating woman," Eunice says. "William has talked about her endlessly."

"Not endlessly," I say good humoredly, though I dare not look at Eunice. Mailer is leaving the party.

"And she's never returned that Italian grammar that William delivered. The rest must be history."

We laugh. Eunice's light merriment sparkles in the air like miniature rocket bursts, and I suddenly have a picture of the two of us, climbing up out of the air-conditioned dive of Louis's one early morning when we were young. It was midsummer, hot and humid, but a shower had sprinkled the pavement around Sheridan Square as we had drunk beer and listened to Peggy Lee on the bar's jukebox. The brief shower had not moderated the heat, but had only stirred up an aroma that came off the steamy cement, as if the gluttonous being of Manhattan had just turned over in satiated torpor. By chance, a checker cab was at the curb, and I hustled Eunice into it and barked our address. By the time we crossed University Place, the deed was being done, and her eyes, in the passing streetlights, had become wide and wildly appreciative of my impetuous ingenuity.

"Well, that grammar," Jones is saying, "fills in part of the puzzle." He looks across the hall, his mouth set curiously. We are quietly attentive.

"Oh dear," Eunice says after a little. "Is that the whir of novel machinery I hear?"

Jones laughs and hugs her again, doesn't drop his arm. "No, it's no use. I've been trying to do her for years, but the nut of the story is so circumstantial that my poor talents cannot make it believable. Every time she'd meet this guy, she would first check into a funeral home over on Madison Avenue to use their facilities. She said it embarrassed her to go to the toilet with him around. I mean even in the Metropolitan." He spread his arms wide with exaggerated amazement. "Well, what was her favorite book again? *Winnie-the-Pooh*?"

"Frank Campbell's," I hear myself say. "That's just over on Madison from the museum. Tommy Dorsey was buried from there," I tell Eunice.

"Yeah, that's the place. Frank Campbell's," Jones says slowly and nods. "She told me she'd go to this place, pay her respects to the deceased, use the john, sign the register on her way out. Put her name and address down to be legit. Then, one day she gets this letter from a Wall Street law firm. Seems that one of the funerals she had attended was that of a rich old geezer who had died with no heirs. No friends. Nobody. Not a dog or a cat. His will ordered that his estate was to be divided among those who came to his layout. Eva was the only one who had showed up—she and her kidneys."

"How much was it?" Eunice's voice flutters like tissue paper.

"She'd just got the letter from the lawyer when I met her, but she had called the firm. Wasn't precise, but well over a million. You can see my problem—just too much chance for fiction."

"And that's how she became a film producer." Eunice puts it all together triumphantly.

"Yeah," Jones says. "She hooked up with that Via Veneto crowd and met this guy Rienzo. We wrote back and forth a little."

"She wrote to you," I say.

"Yeah, when *The Message from Alice* came out. So, back and forth a few times. She and the Italian had a kind of spirtual-artistic relationship, from what she said. Seems he swung both ways. But it suited her. Hey, that's my old lady over there. She's been looking for me, I bet. The gal in the purple pants. I've got a few years up on her, but so far staying in step." His boyish face fails in its attempt at a leer. He is just too good-humored.

His wife is a statuesque, black-haired woman of about thirty, and she is talking with large-gestured abandon to an entranced Robert Stone. "She's lovely," Eunice says, and I must agree.

"Hey!" Jones has suddenly remembered something. "A bunch of us are going over to Nan Talese's. Why don't you come along?"

"I think not," I say. "But thanks." Eunice looks disappointed but quickly renews her cheerful look. Jones's wife is making what seems to be Boy Scout semaphore signals in our direction.

"I have to go," he says. "The worst part is that Eva turned up with lumps. Here." His broad hand smoothed down the sweater he wore beneath his jacket.

"Oh, my." Eunice put one hand to her lips.

"Yeah, bad news. Right after Rienzo's first big hit. About the pocketbook."

"La Borsetta." I supply the name.

"That's the one. Eva wrote me about the operation. Even whimsical about that. Falsies for every occasion, she said. Well, you remember how she was. Quite a gal." His wife has been making more signals. People are leaving in large groups. The bar is closed. "It's been great," Jones is saying. "Let's keep in touch." He shakes my hand and kisses Eunice delicately near one ear, then saunters across the hall to his wife, who hugs one of his arms, wriggles with happiness enough for both of them.

"Well," Eunice says after a moment. "I'm famished and not ashamed to admit it. I feel like something Italian. Let's go to Julio's—it's on the way home. For some scaloppine. How about it?"

The caterers have begun to clean up the remains of the party. Plastic cups clatter upon the marble floor, and somebody is whistling a happy melody. Just at the door, Eunice suddenly stops and turns to me. "Oh, William," she says and kisses me on the mouth. When she pulls back, her eyes glisten. The low illumination of the place is reflected and somehow charged by her tears, in which I have just seen my mean ambition and small desires.

The Plagiarist

Carlos cannot change the typewriter ribbon. The narrow material has snarled and become jammed against the carrier's small gates. One of the spools has come undone, spiraling to the floor like a streamer thrown during a perverse funeral. But he will not change his habits; his wife has urged him to use a computer. "It is quieter," Jane has said on more than one occasion.

"*Mierda,*" he mutters, then he shouts, "Jane!"

The house is silent. Gulls screech far down at the bay. The boys have gone sailing, and his wife is in the side yard, turning in the morning sunlight like a plump *perdiz*. The pads of his short fingers have become soiled by the ribbon's ink, and he can plainly see the swirls in his skin, read the lines of resemblance to his father's thick stubby fingers, and then, as if the sound has been waiting to be reproduced in the maze of his fingerprint, he hears his father swearing over *la maquinaria*. The tractor and combine were forever breaking down on their farm in Guanajuato.

"Jane—please." His plea is strained and just a little impatient.

Drops of sweat have appeared on the backs of his hands to glisten among the coarse black hairs that grow there. Peasant hands shaped for ordinary work, rough jobs that demanded strength and yet were done with elegance, sometimes made clumsy by the inventions of men with more supple fingers. These same hands wedged down the typewriter's throat had made him famous by the delicate manner they had arranged English and Spanish, by the nuances they wove around the lives of men and women.

"Bastardo." The ribbon has snared his fingers completely. "Jane. I need you. Please." The plea becomes a command.

Also, the way women had pressed themselves into these square hands of an *indio* had always amazed him. Sometimes they seemed to fear their touch, perhaps afraid of their coarse strength, yet they would come almost as penitents. Yes, *martyrs* would be too strong a word, for what after all was sacrificed? It had been so with his wife.

They had been sitting on a bench behind the Palace of Fine Art in Mexico City. She had been a student then, a young American in sandals with a notebook on her lap, and she had taken his hands and placed them on the front of her blouse. She was pledging herself, he thought, and he remembers looking up into the heavy canopy of palms overhead, too astonished to meet her eyes until the heavy embroidery of her blouse snagged the skin of his fingers.

These days, both men and women come to ask his help in shaping their language to turn the ordinary facts of their lives into fiction they can appreciate, and sometimes, a woman takes his hands and rubs her face into the cinnamon-colored palms—a curious anointment before she gives him the rest of herself. Carlos sometimes wonders if these women expect him to reshape their bodies as he tries to reshape their prose, though the perfection of a limb that sometimes turns within his hands can have only been milled in a dream. Their behavior always takes him by surprise; his attitude would surprise them, for they think him worldly and expectant.

"Mierda. Estoy harto!" Carlos jumps up, knocking the swivel chair so it slams against the metal file cabinet against his study's wall. The kitchen

screen door has opened and cracks shut. Bare feet pad across the linoleum floor. "Jane." At last, she has come.

The sun has made her almost as dark as he. Long black hair falls straight and below her shoulders, and her breasts are momentarily naked for she is retying the top of her bikini and lifting her breasts into the scraps of fabric. The stalk of celery she holds in one hand is starkly white against her deep tan. She is the mother of his children, he thinks, but were it not for the light color of her eyes, she could be his youngest sister. He gestures toward the tangle of ribbon on the typewriter's front. "Look."

"Oh, Carlos, what have you done?" Her voice is sympathetic and carries just a seasoning of the hard Massachusetts accent that had so intrigued him when they sat beneath the palms behind the Palace of Fine Art. How could such metallic notes be struck within such soft flesh? "If you could only bring yourself to use a computer like everyone else," she says and hands him the celery.

"But I would miss the clack-clack. Brick falling upon brick to build the structure, the house of words."

"Yes, yes," Jane says. "Building the adobe. I've heard all that." She has bent over the worktable to unravel the mess. Her fingers move swiftly and sure.

"Not too old, I hope," he says and steps up behind her.

"Now back off, if you want me to fix this."

Carlos stands to one side and seeks the reverie that absorbed him this morning before all this trouble began. He had woken to a line of poetry, and he raises the celery stalk to silently beat time to the rhythm of the language.

Es un desierto circular el mundo.

When he had unwisely decided to change the ribbon, a story was about to reveal itself. First came the image of a desert, the high mesa of Guanajuato during a drought, and how his father stood facing the distant Sierra, where the winds gathered. The man had been both a sentry and a witness to the wind's attack upon his dried up farmland, and his eyes were slits against the sting and slash, as if he had to keep track of these winds, as if, were he to miss the end of them, they would circle around to blow off the topsoil forever.

And just before Carlos had made the mistake of removing the ribbon spools from their spindles, other figures had projected themselves onto the blank sheet of paper that rose so boldly from the platen to challenge him. His brothers and sisters, the grandmother who had raised them all, and even that old dog who had been his special care. He saw himself appear on the paper, the figure of a small boy holding out a pie tin, round and rusted, as if to collect some of that swirling dust, to keep some of that world from being sucked into the sky and leaving the clay beneath their feet picked clean. The story would be quite different from the wry love stories that had made him fashionable and that, in a way, had brought him to this coastal village in New England—far from Mexico.

Then, the ribbon became tangled.

He could no longer help his father, even if he could put down the words that would catch the ambient light of that past. English, as a foreign language, no longer surprised him, but these days he had to work hard to fabricate the charm that had once been artless, for which his fiction was noted, so how could he do honor to those modest people?

Jane has shifted her feet, and the pose thrusts her right hip and torso into a Hellenic cant. The skimpy bikini covers just a small part of her buttocks and the thin string of her halter marks her coffee-colored back. With the celery stalk, Carlos conducts the line of poetry once more, *es un desierto circular el mundo*, while picturing the roundness of his wife's breasts swaying over the typewriter and how the small gold crucifix hangs from her neck, surely a gratuitous object of worship.

He relishes the small roll of flesh that circles her waist and that goes around, he knows, to inform the slight swell of her belly. She is always going on diets, and his uncritical appreciation of her figure sometimes angers her. Or brings up anger. "If you like fat so much," she turned on him once, "how come these students you screw are always skinny?"

She has rewound the one spool and neatly snaps it in place and now holds the other one in both hands to undo the twists his clumsiness had made. Her face is tense, the expression both studious and young, though a different care has straightened her spine. She stands up stiffly. She has felt his look and registered all he has been thinking. Her smooth skin has measured the light in his eyes with a peculiar photosensitivity. Carlos sometimes wondered if women are born with a sensitivity to men's eyes, perhaps a defensive mechanism that comes with the gender. Or if not born with it, they become conditioned to the feel of men's eyes from an early age, starting with fathers and brothers, then strangers and lovers. Their skin learns to interpret the play of men's eyes with the same facility as their ears understand the whispers or shouts that often accompany these stares.

"Leave me alone if you want this fixed," Jane says without shifting her concentration.

Carlos clears his throat with a mollient clucking meant to soften her mood, but she turns abruptly to face him. The crucifix lies in the valley of her brown breasts like the wreck of a small plane. "If you want some action, why don't you go to that little cookie you have stashed down at the wharf?"

"Which cookie is that, my darling?"

"That little waitress you've been shacking up with in the afternoon. I read that story you just sent in, another of your piquant interludes. Do you think I can't understand where you get your ideas? But Carlos, you have really hurt me this time." The small study offers no room for such a confrontation. He cannot back away. "You have really hurt me," Jane continues. "You brought this girl here this summer to my town. This is *my* town."

"Ah, that person. I only got her a job at the fish restaurant on the pier. She's on a scholarship and must earn some of her expenses for the winter. She has little money." He pauses, but the suggestion that there are people who must work for their money no longer embarrasses her. "And as for the story," his eyes grow large, "you must know by now that it is all invented. A fantasy. *Todo inventarté.*"

"*Inventarté,* my ass. We're all fair game for your so-called invention, I know that well enough. Now get out of here and let me finish this job. Where's the type cleaner?—these fonts are filthy too. Go on now, get out."

Carlos walks into the next room and then the kitchen. These rooms look out upon a small yard enclosed by a very high privet hedge that has grown wild and untrimmed to give a scraggly privacy. The branches trap fragments of the morning light, pieces of a mirror—he thinks—that has lost its image.

Somewhere in the circular desert of this world there might be a grain of new truth that has not been blown away, not cast beyond the horizon, that he might catch and hold in his hands—a small star that would burn through him to leave him luminous and clear and able to translate a simple feeling onto paper. What is the next line? He looked the poem up while having his first cup of tea and before he sat down at the typewriter.

El cielo esta cerrado y el inferno vacío.

Truly, Paz must have brought back that stylish paradox from Paris, café talk, for it could not have grown from the poor soil of a *campesino*. For if heaven is closed and hell empty, what happened to the figures he saw on the paper in his typewriter? Where would the lovers he wrote about go? Has he set them in motion only for them to embrace in an endless reel, and never to rest? He looks for something ordinary, a commonplace to appreciate in the front yard.

A small clump of jonquils, the lemony blooms shriveled, thrusts up unexpectedly from the sandy soil in the center of the plot. Jane cannot remember planting the bulbs there, so the flower's appearance every spring has always surprised them. One of the boy's bicycles lies to one side. Carlos uses it more than his son these days, pedaling shakily around the seaport to the store or the post office. Or down to the wharf.

Someone has just passed on the other side of the hedge. People often cut across the dunes near their house on their way to the bay beach. But he sees the figure pause, then stop at the picket fence, and, with a casualness Carlos finds insulting, reach over and flip open the latch. This moon-faced gringo shows an easy know-how with their gate that implies all gates— every door of the civilized world—are accessible to him; all entries are easily forced. He could flip them open while thinking of sundry matters. The gate swings back with a slap against the post, undoubtedly loosening the screws with which Carlos refastened the old hinges just last week.

"H-sst—Jane—Jane." He speaks like a bandit.

"What?" she answers loudly.

"Shh-shh." He puts a finger to his lips and motions her to the window.

"Why, it's—" She recognizes the intruder.

"I don't want to see him. Shh! I'm not here. Yes. I have gone sailing with the boys."

"But that's—"

"Do as I say." Carlos tiptoes into his study and carefully pulls the door shut just as the screen door in the kitchen vibrates with an unseemly rattle. The beach house makes them vulnerable, exposed, and Jane has often protected him by lying to people who just drop by, other writers or former students. This morning's visitor is one of the latter, a serious young man whose adulation has become a nuisance.

The typewriter is ready to go. The new ribbon snakes cleverly through the several stiles and guides, and the spools sit confidently on their posts. Affection for his wife surges through him, rising from his gratitude, and this warmth attacks the cold block that has sat on his imagination. The desert of the blank page in the typewriter's roller has been moistened by freshets of words that begin to appear. Figures move around again, and the old dog—yes, he would use the old dog—starts to run in this direction and then another on the scent of a narrative that will lead him to where the story has been buried all these years. Renew his citizenship, he thinks. But he dares not touch the typewriter.

He hears their visitor say he is sorry that Carlos is not at home. The young man speaks as if he is addressing an athletic event. He's one of those tall, blond Anglos who get pinker in the sun, with a nose like a *tamale*.

How unattractive his voice sounds. What else is he saying to Jane? Carlos listens intently.

He recognized the young writer as something of a leach when he showed up at the workshop at Bread Loaf, but he put up with the pestering because Jane expressed a liking for him. She has just said something, and chairs scrape the kitchen floor. Carlos can't believe they are sitting down, but clearly that has happened. No doubt Jane has offered the fellow a cup of coffee, and he has accepted. His wife is always trapping herself by issuing invitations not meant to be accepted, an agreeable convention that is too often taken seriously by people who know no better. It was almost Jamesian—no, something by Edith Wharton—and Carlos plays with the idea for a story. But he would have to remember it, because if he leans forward to reach the pencil and paper on his desk, the chair will squeak. He has been meaning to oil the swivel all summer.

The small window next to his desk faces the wall of a woodshed, and the shadow of the house's roofline is etched upon its weathered strakes by the midmorning sun. Every morning he has worked here—sometimes only sat here—until this pattern on the woodshed wall has lost its fine edge and he knew the sun would be high overhead. He could tell by this measurement—a Mayan inheritance, he would joke to himself—that several hours were left of the morning. Carefully he places a finger on the key for the letter *o* and presses down. The type font lifts like the head of a newly born serpent emerging from its shell to lightly kiss the surface of the paper, then just as slowly withdraws and resumes its place in the nest. Just then, the donkey bray of a laugh comes from the kitchen, surprisingly joined by Jane's fruity amusement. This visit may take longer than he has feared.

His study is small. Jane instructed him that it had been an extra bed-room added on cell-like to sleep an aged cousin in some distant generation. Within its tight dimensions have been fitted his typing table, work table, the swivel chair, two small bookcases and the metal file cabinet. They are the interlocked pieces of a puzzle that it pleased him to resolve every morn-ing. The one window makes up much of the third wall, and pictures hang on either side. These include photographs of Juárez and Zapata as well as scenes from his village of Delicias. The reproduction of a mural by Diego Rivera is thumbtacked to one side. As a youth, he had been in confession-als larger, and this comparison has become an old joke between them, that he did not write in this room so much as make confessions. He presses his ear to the door, for it has become abruptly silent in the kitchen. Both seem to be whispering, but the sound could be a breeze through the pine trees at the rear of the lot.

Now that this fellow has shown up, amiably having coffee and sitting with Jane in her bikini, Carlos recognizes that he has been expecting him. The young man wrote him long, unasked-for letters, sent him copies of his stories, and Carlos was initially happy to participate. It was the usual exchange between a younger and an established writer, the customary interplay between master and apprentice—offerings paid the muses. The boy had talent, but then, they all had talent; yet, Carlos had been compli-mentary, supportive. Then, last spring, that disturbing note scrawled across a page torn out of *Esquire*. "Great story—where *do* you get your ideas?"

Well, as he often told his students, there are only so many ideas and the same set of human facts. Academics were always writing books describing the two or seven or twelve basic plots, but it is what each writer makes of the facts that made the difference. Moreover, everyone borrows—literature is enriched by theft—and the nature of workshops and writing conferences makes for a kind of casual swapping of styles and language—a *partouze,* the French might call it—to produce a progeny with a common parentage. True, one of the stories he was sent—it had appeared in a small quarterly— did resemble the one he was to publish in *Esquire* a year later, for both concerned a couple attempting to renew their relationship by revisiting a place important to their history. But there the similarity ended. His story featured his familiar cast of lovers—older man and younger woman—and the student's piece was about a father and son. Not at all the same.

"Ho-ho-hah." The laughter booms in the kitchen. "I see—I see." What does that intruder see? He sees Jane's sumptuous breasts. He is watching her mouth—pleasantly shaped and good mannered. He sees the white enameled tabletop and the tea bag he left on a saucer earlier. Carlos listens intently, leans forward slowly to put his ear toward the door. Silence. He imagines Jane waiting politely and patiently for the fellow to finish his coffee and leave. The light through the screen door would strike his wife's eyes and they would reflect silvery flecks of pearl. Something clatters to the floor—a spoon perhaps.

Usually by this part of the morning, he might have two pages down, and he would get up to walk to the kitchen to make another cup of tea. He is not thirsty, but the habit denied him makes him clench his fists. He could starve to death in here while that Yanqui jabbers. He still has the celery. The semicircle of Jane's small bite has been copied onto its ribbed surface. He lifts the vegetable to his lips and fits her indentation against his large front teeth. He grimaces the way Pedro Armendáriz used to do in the movies—a wide smile with very large white teeth. "Pedro Armendáriz. *Me llamo Carlos,*" he whispers and takes a large bite. The celery cracks like a rifle shot, the limb of a tree snapping, and he presses it against the roof of his mouth. Nothing from the kitchen. Carefully, he works his jaws. If he chews very slowly, the celery will last a long time.

Jane has not given him away, and he will write a new story for her. This story will be the truth of what happened on the wharf, because she always misreads his stories, and these artless interpretations have always amused him until now. He will call his editor in New York, pull back the story, and send him another that is more truthful.

Because fact turned to fiction when the man's figure paused on the outside stairway rising to the small room above the marine supply store. Up to that point, the account was truthful. Yes, the small landing had pots of red geraniums. The man was aware of his exposure, anyone could see him on the stairs, but his desire had drugged him so he had become insensate to surveillance. Large dark horseflies drowsily worked their way up the sun-baked shingles beside him. Then the girl's laughter made him hesitate halfway up. He recognized the open-throated timbre of her amusement. That braggadocio sound of a Shakespeare heroine had initially attracted him, but there in the open, the sunlight illuminated something cold and calculated in her voice, and he leaned against the stair railing to listen. Without seeing her laugh, without the appearance matching the sound, the separation of eye from ear startled him.

"That's just beautiful," he hears Jane exclaim in the kitchen.

"Do you think so?" the fellow replies.

Carlos knows that a manuscript must lie between them on the smooth white tabletop, an offering. They always brought manuscripts. Why could they not bring cake or a bottle of wine? Some fruit? Carlos carefully bites into the celery. But of course, he is responsible for such a gift, this tender of words. He had presented to all of them the example of himself holding out his circular fictions to catch reality.

But his stories were admired for their tidy conclusions rounded on ironic pictures. So, he had turned the man around on the stair landing and let him walk down and across to the wharf parking lot, where he had left the bicycle leaning against the ice machine. The fiction continued. He waited there until dark and a light went on in the small room above him. Carlos had him watch until the light went out, and then he pushed the bicycle away. The bicycle had no light on it and would be dangerous to ride at night. The town police might stop him, but they would recognize him, and he would explain to them that he had warned his son more than once about the dangers of riding the bike without a light or reflectors. To do so was not only dangerous but probably against the law.

The broad, Indian features of Juárez keep a quizzical expression, as if the photographer had asked el Presidente a stupid question just as the shutter clicked. "Wait a minute," Jane says in the kitchen and a chair scrapes on the floor. Is she getting more coffee for the gringo? How can she do that? Carlos judiciously selects a yellow leaf from the celery stalk, places it upon his tongue and closes his mouth. He stretches his mouth wide. My name is Pedro Armendáriz. It looks like a long siege. The line of shadow on the woodshed wall is losing its definition. He has always been taken aback by the quick familiarity of American women, though he does not disdain their frankness.

He slowly aligns the typewriter's carriage with the machine's square body. He plays a nervy game, gliding the carriage within a hair of the position that would trip the little bell to signal the margin. He wins. He neatens the stack of copy paper on the worktable. The unmarked paper in the platen becomes the screen he used to set up in the church hall in Delicias that would become crowded with faces and vistas that became real in the dark.

For, in fact, the young woman had been alone, and she greeted him when he reached the stop of the stairs. She shaped a kiss over the telephone's mouthpiece and waved him to a chair with the hairbrush in her other hand. When she paused to listen, she stroked her hair with the brush, pensive caesuras within the line of her own conversation. She and the other person seemed to be talking about a mutual acquaintance, someone he did not know.

Her desk had been next to him. On it was a laptop, a glass spiked with pencils, and a dictionary. It was a student's desk. The mirror over the bureau was posted with a cartoon clipped from a magazine, the picture of a young man she said was her brother, two postcards, and several lines of Unamuno in his typescript. A very large pillow, the shape and color of a sunburst, rose from the bed's chenille bolster.

As he watched, the leaps and runs of her talk became dearly familiar to him. The sentences seemed to go in all directions at once, made more comprehensible by their energy than by their words, and her movements displayed a further fluency. Her bare legs stretched, touched at the knees, took up different stances, for she always seemed to carry on these phone conversations standing up as if the excitement that charged their ordinary subjects could not be tolerated sitting down. The same passionate intensity of her laughter, singled out like a nucleus in a laboratory, had startled him on the stairway outside. Separated from the innocent sprawl of her gestures, the sound had become superficial and hateful.

He thought irony would melt like a sliver of ice in this room, nearly open to the sky. He felt he had biked for many miles rather than just from the center of town and most of that downhill. The young woman continued to talk with her back to him, the telephone cord wound around her. Her enthusiasm remained undiminished, her zest soared, and he sensed that if he tried to imitate her passion, kidnap the zeal of it, he would fumble and become overwhelmed.

When she finally hung up the phone and turned to him eagerly and curiously refreshed, she found him crying. He was a man not afraid to show tears, though he might sometimes be a little wary of their cause and meaning. She became serious and more beautiful as she sat down on the end of the bed, uncertain of what to do about him; her eyes reflected her dilemma. He had become an embarrassment in the afternoon—he could understand that—and she lifted the hairbrush and continued to slowly brush her hair.

Jane would not believe this story. She did not like the other one either, but she had believed in its neatness and invention. What would his editor say? "It is charming, Carlos, but you do the other irony much more effectively." He turns back to the typewriter and admires its sensible construction, the regular logic of its design. The kitchen is still. Have they left—walked out of the house, arm in arm and across the dunes to look for a straight line in the sand? He lifts his hands but dares not strike any of the keys. Hell must surely be empty—all of it is here in this crowded room. But if he opens the door, he might meet their faces raised to him like school chums interrupted in their homework. The fellow's expression would shift to one of amusement and then scorn. His suspicions would be confirmed. What stories this guy could tell. He would be invited to workshops just to relate them. He might even put it on paper and win a prize.

Carlos places the last bit of celery in his mouth and chews it thoroughly. A murmur lifts in the kitchen, and he presses his ear against the metal case of the large typewriter as if the machine could articulate their words. It has never failed him before, but now it is silent, and he is trapped in this room by the truth that awaits him outside the door.

Double Wedding Ring

Again, she told her husband that she had to go into the city to find material for the quilt, to rummage in remnant shops for scraps she would bring back to trim and stitch into the pattern called Double Wedding Ring.

It was to be a very large quilt, and on its frame it took up much of the space of the small dining room of their apartment. They ate all their meals in the kitchen anyway, they no longer entertained, and they actually preferred the cozy and convenient breakfast nook that looked out over the neat lawns and manicured shrubbery of the grounds.

"You're never going to finish that, are you?" her husband sometimes said with a patient good-humor that always put her on the edge between two lines of reply. The affection in his scold would center her feelings for him, and she might kiss him and muss the hair that fell over his collar or she would turn to some mindless chore, a little sorry for his patronizing tone. No, she would say to herself, it will never be finished. Never.

So in the city, she spent several very happy hours sorting through piles of cotton fabric in two stores in the city's warehouse district, near the river. She had certain colors in mind. One was a Dresden blue—not too busy— and she came across just the right match early on. Other finds were gathered and then, as if to treat herself, she uncovered an outrageous vermilion with black dots, like a slice of watermelon, that she was convinced would excite a rather prim alignment taking shape in one corner of the quilt. A delicate rose also caught her eye, though she had no idea where she would apply this fragment, but she promised a place for its freshness.

So, by the time she reached the hotel, she was humming to herself happily. Her morning's success, the very ease with which she had supported the lie she had given her husband, somehow granted her guiltless pleasures in whatever the rest of the day would hold. At the same time, she was aware that this good fortune with all its random idleness and sweetness could not be completely pulled over the deception of the afternoon.

As usual, the door of the hotel room was slightly ajar, a tact she had appreciated in him from the beginning. She would not have to knock to gain entrance to her infidelity. Also as always, he had ordered little sandwiches of salmon and cucumber with a pot of tea for her and coffee for him. From the beginning, he had always included little snacks in their adultery, but he had been drinking decaf for several years now. He rose to greet her, leaving the baseball game muted on the television behind him. They embraced.

This was the worst part for her—not the leave-taking later, but this greeting that carried the unalterable farewell within it. She cried silently as he pressed her to himself with long arms whose embrace was nearly painful. Tears gathered in the corners of her eyes and then became absorbed in the crisp, clean-smelling terrain of his shirtfront. She observed the grayish hairs around his ear. He needed a trim. Why she cried after all these years bemused her, and she let it go as some sort of a reflex appropriate to the situation, a matter of form perhaps. She cried for their years together.

In the early days of their affair, her tears were rinsed in anger. She had raged against the corny melodrama of their circumstances, the outright injustice that forced them to meet in hotel rooms. Indeed, that thought would make her laugh too; they had outlasted two hotels—one had been torn down and the other had become a condominium. Love or affection, their earlier lust, she no longer could tell the difference or where one had become the other, and the routine of their affair eventually had comforted her and soothed the anger. They had this secret, at least, when they would slip out of their daily apparel and become different selves. So her crying had become part of that ritual, as if it were expected of her role.

"I must look a sight." She broke away and glanced quickly in the mirror over the bureau. It wasn't a very long look, for she knew how she looked; moreover, she carried within herself how she should look, how she looked when they first met. She had never been beautiful, but she had fine eyes and an appealing, near giddy expression when she smiled that drew attention to the pensive mote in her eyes. She liked to think of herself as neat—neatly put together and modestly proportioned—not a knockout, but in all probability, long-lasting.

"You look swell," he said. He had stooped to busy himself with cups and saucers and to give her a little time to collect herself. She wiped around her eyes and blew her nose with a tissue from the holder on the bureau and then slipped out of her shoes. She took up her position against some pillows at the head of the bed and crossed her ankles. He handed her a cup of tea with lemon and an arrangement of the tiny sandwiches on a plate.

"Marvelous. Just what I needed," she said. "I'm famished. How's the game?"

"The Mets have bought it. And you—did you find what you were looking for?"

"A great success. Right off and with some unexpected bonuses as well." The tea was especially satisfying, but the bread of the sandwiches was a little dry. He may have ordered room service too soon. His practice wasn't all that busy these days, and he may have checked into the room early. She pictured him sitting before the television set waiting for her and changed the subject of her imagination. The game was in its final innings. She had been about to describe the riotous crimson swatch she had turned over when he turned to her.

"What's the name of this one again?"

"Double Wedding Ring."

"Yes—that's right, Double Wedding Ring." The name seemed to amuse him.

"It's one of the classic patterns—very traditional." She explained how the rings interlocked to make a chain, circles endlessly interlocked and turning their motley circumferences across the white field of the quilt. He nodded slowly, listening with some interest to her description and not for the first time. He was still very handsome. His hair had gone completely white, but his eyebrows remained dark, giving his expression a brooding intensity that bursts of boyishness could easily rout.

That combination had been her ruin. He had made a dark study of her, methodically opening the secret drawers within her to sort and identify the contents but with a cheerfulness, an unfounded optimism that made her trust him. She had recognized him as a city man, practiced in the delicacies of ravishment and the deft setting up of protocols that preceded a breath-stopping chaos. She had known what was happening to her, and she also knew that it might not ever happen again.

He had come equipped with the tale of an invalid wife, stock material for a womanizer; yet, she was to discover he was telling the truth. In fact, he always told the truth, which may have been his ultimate strategy for seduction. And then she recognized that he had become as spellbound by her as she was taken with him and that they had unintentionally flown into the same cage. Why her, she sometimes asked him as they lay in the sequestered gloom of a hotel room? Why had he given up the stunning, sophisticated women who had passed through his hands with all the silky negligence of the exquisite scarves they wore around their throats?

"Why you?" The question always seemed to astonish him. He never had an answer, so he would fabricate silly responses meant to tease the doubts she had about herself as they covered his own inability to answer her. "Because you were an easy lay. In from the suburbs looking for adventure at the craft fair and with that all-togetherness that begged to be undone, button by button." Halfway through such burlesques she would invariably enfold him, her naked limbs tangling his, her fingers and lips smothering his words, smoothing the harshness of them as she soothed their sound over the tender heart she knew was hers.

She came to the end of the description of the quilt and wriggled her toes, recrossed her feet. She knew he had stopped listening to her.

"It's over," he said at last.

"When?"

"A week Tuesday."

"I'm so very sorry," she said, and she really was sorry. Unaccountably, she felt a grief that measured the death of his wife. The heavy drapery at the window muffled the blare of car horns on the street below. One corner of the bureau top had a small chip out of it. She carefully set her cup down on the saucer.

He had taken one of her feet in his hands, to massage the instep, gently press the articulation of the ankle as if it might have been his own invention. "You'd think I'd be ready for it by now, wouldn't you?" Then he turned his head aside. A tremor ran across his shoulders. She looked at the very poor watercolor of a summer garden that hung on the opposite wall. "Damn," he said and then softer, "damn."

He was a quiet man who generally bore the circumstances of his life without too much complaint—only a little sardonic humor now and then. In any event, he had never bored her with the melancholy details as some men might have done, and once she knew of his wife's degenerative condition, he rarely spoke about it. Nor did she say much about her husband. In that first tryst, once the clothes came off, the truth had come out, so why bother going over the same material? Yes, her husband could be dry, and as an academic, the distinction in scholarship he had claimed was revealed in his retirement to be only a creation of department politics. But he was a good man, and he had been good to her. More important, his performance as a father and recently as a grandfather had delighted her. More than delighted her.

As their children grew, her husband had seemed to grow into a further maturity, one that eschewed pretensions and cobbled reputation and that embellished their family with a richness she became fond of. Odd, she often wondered, how this transformation in her husband had also enhanced her and made her happy as she took a part. More than happy; taking up this new script, as it were, she read her lines with conviction and sincerity. But all of that had nothing to do with why she was here in this hotel room. From the beginning, that script was irrelevant to the scenes she entered in so many hotel rooms to find this man, who was now caressing her feet, waiting for her with an eagerness only matched by the rush in her heart.

"May I join you?" He had stepped out of his tasseled loafers and stood by the bed, pulling off his tie.

"Please do," she replied, marveling at the number of times they had made this exchange, the different tones of its expression. In the early days, the courtesy was extended as she often lay in a stew of desire. Not knowing where to look at him but always coming back to his sprung excitement, which she knew to be her doing—that she was the cause of it, and this discovery only heated the pool within her more. Today, his gesture drew an indolent amusement from her as she remembered the history of the request and all its playful invitations. Mannered as always, he could have been asking to share her seat on a bus, though the glint in his eyes was devilish. She shifted to one side on the bed and plumped up some pillows for him.

"That's a terrible painting," he said, once settled beside her. "Why is that painting so bad? What's wrong with it?"

"It's the light in it," she said. "The light is all one, no variation."

"Yes, I see what you mean. No shadings." The flickering glow of the television made sporadic forays into the dim room. A player was being interviewed; the game was over. "You used to paint. Why did you give it up?" he asked.

"Because I wasn't very good."

"You were painting when we met."

"No, I was into ceramics then. Tiles. The painting came later."

"Whatever did you do with that ghastly decal of that singer you were going to make into some kind of hot plate?"

"That was Vic Damone, and it was a splendidly awful hot plate. I gave it to my sister for Christmas. She still uses it. Lucky for you it was so dreadful. Its very tackiness excited your snobbery and drew you into my clutches." She turned on her side and hugged him.

"Trapped by the commonplace, is that it?"

"You better believe it," she said and raised her face to receive his kiss. Their lips joined easily.

"But I really wasn't looking for anything that day."

"Sure you were; prowling the craft fair to scan the prospects."

"No, remember? I wanted to get a doll for my daughter. You helped me pick out that Snoopy doll."

"So you asked any female to help you out."

"Not just any female."

"You might as well have said, 'What about a quick one?'" She felt a little shameless and giggled. "In fact, I'm not sure that you didn't say that."

"Well we did, didn't we?"

"Yes, we did," she replied abruptly thoughtful.

They had revisited that first meeting many times. It was an old album they would take out and pore over as if to find a picture they had missed before, a snapshot that would explain once and for all what had happened to them. The plain evidence of that moment, however many times reviewed, never gave up a clue to their ensuing dilemma. It had been the last day of the fair, a Saturday, so the doors were closing at midafternoon. Around them, the tumult gradually dwindled; the sea of hobbyists that had surrounded them calmed and disappeared. Exhibit booths were being knocked down. The gay frippery of the exhibitions was reduced to tatters of colored paper, and cardboard and waste bins were crammed with crushed and bundled displays. The high ceiling of the convention hall loomed above them, suddenly no longer obscured, and the crash of hammers and the whine of power saws came from every direction.

They strolled the aisles of this destruction, she with her shopping bag of tiles and decals and he clasping the stuffed dog to his chest. They had come to the center of the enormous space, feeling very much alone—themselves on display, though ignored by the workmen around them. He invited her to have some coffee.

"My train leaves just after five," she replied, knowing she was about to do something she had never done before.

Even then, this strange man had called down to room service after they had made love and ordered up some sandwiches. He liked to eat, and she found this appetite appealing as she had found the other one overwhelming. Even now, he had brought a plate of the salmon sandwiches to the bed and carefully savored one before putting the rest on the floor when she showed no interest in them. "Does the TV bother you?" he asked.

"No, it seems homey, like a little fireplace."

His arm had passed around her, and she lay against him one hand lightly resting on the front of his trousers. She saw them in the mirror above the bureau opposite the bed, a couple posed and positioned for the next move. The act itself had become a genial reference to the forces that had once driven them so furiously. Their image appeared to her like one of those shaggy couples in a Rowlandson print—*The Roué at Rest* might be an appropriate title.

"What's funny?" he asked.

"Nothing. Nothing's funny." She pressed herself into him. He squeezed her waist; one hand sized the curve of her hip.

"I'm free now," he said after a while. When she said nothing, he continued. "I mean I could travel. Go somewhere for a little bit. Venice, for instance. What about Venice? I've always wanted to see Venice."

"How am I to get away?"

"Venice is famous for its glassblowers."

"You've got it all worked out, I see."

"You could say you wanted to study glassblowing."

"That isn't funny." She raised up and looked him in the face.

"No, it's not. I'm sorry. But here we are at last." He turned and kissed her on the mouth. She tasted something a little sour on his tongue, perhaps the flavor of the capers that had spiced the salmon. She surrendered to his urgency, pleased by it and just a little curious as to what the two of them would make of it. Moreover, her practical side reminded her that he had paid for the room and they should use it to the best of their ability.

When she surfaced from the usual half slumber, she saw that it had grown late and that she must move quickly. She eyed him sprawled on the bed as she restored her clothing. A soft whistling rose from his pursed mouth. She considered leaving him like that, easing out the door without saying the hateful words of farewell. Carefully, she ran water in the bathroom sink to wash her face and then she restored her makeup. She inspected her reflection in the mirror, thinking she looked rather ordinary.

When she returned to the room, he was sitting on the edge of the bed and pulling his shirt down over his head. With a pang, she noted this procedure. He never unbuttoned his dress shirts completely and would pull them up and off himself and then back on as a boy would do with a sweatshirt, pushing his arms through the sleeves in a sort of rebellion against fastenings.

"We will be different." His voice was quiet.

"Yes. Probably. I don't know." She attacked the backs of her knees and behind her ears with quick sprays of cologne from a small atomizer. He had once called that a whore's application, and she hadn't been offended, but amused, even curiously flattered. She worried her hair with a brush, then tossed it into her purse. "I've got to fly. I'll miss my train." She came to him quickly and put one knee on the bed to lean toward him. She took his face in her hands and kissed him slowly. His large hands held her torso capably, and one of them slipped up her blouse to cup a breast. "Always copping a last feel," she said against his mouth.

"Always."

"Thanks for lunch. I'll call you." She moved away swiftly, not daring to say more. He waved casually and tucked his shirt into his trousers and closed up the zipper. A news program had begun on the television, apparently about some incident in China. She closed the door.

A light rain had begun when she burst through the hotel's revolving door, and she was worried about getting a taxi. She tucked the bag of material and her purse under one arm and ran down to the curb, the other arm raised high, fingers pointing. She ignored the doorman who seemed immobilized by the whistle stuck in his mouth. Luckily, a taxi swung over from the flow of avenue traffic, and she jumped in. She felt lithe and young and just a little lightheaded. She was eager to get back to the quilt and to see how the material she was bringing home would work in the pattern. She was pretty sure the colors would be perfect. She was also eager to get back to her husband now.

The cab had stopped for a traffic light. A couple stood on the corner, hesitant to cross. The young woman held an umbrella over the two of them while pressing her other arm down along the front of her blouse and slacks as if to shield herself. This reference to modesty made on a street corner in the rain could just as easily have been made in a darkened room. Or, the young woman might only be uncomfortable standing with this young man in the rain, not knowing how to say good-bye—without hurting his feelings—one arm pressed against herself and minding the traffic.

How the Indians Buried Their Dead

When the conference adjourns, the men relax and their talk turns to personal matters. Some swivel their chairs to face the large window, a vault of glass that keeps the city's skyline. Clouds, the color of gunmetal and perhaps as heavy, hang below the top floors of the skyscraper, their edges traced in gold by the weak afternoon sun.

On second thought, the clouds remind him of thick puddings baked in a faulty oven so their tops become toasty brown as the rest stays gray and lumpish. He has not been out of the building since he arrived for the meeting; all living, entertainment as well as their business, has been conducted inside it. However, he knows what it would be like on the other side of this large pane of glass, down there in the city. He can feel and smell the heat out there, like the memory of an old blanket in a summer attic.

"But it's interesting you were born here," the man at his elbow replies. "It must be strange to come back here like this and overlook the old hometown from way up here. Haven't been back since you left? And when was that?"

No, he will say, he doesn't remember exactly when he left, though he remembers the sort of day it was, what time it was, and other details. It was many years ago. In fact, he now recalls, he had been sent to visit relatives while his parents disposed of the house and packed their possessions. They moved to another city, and he had been sent away to visit cousins to ease the shock. He remembers the details of that leave-taking but not when it happened. The man beside him accepts a cup of tea and a small sandwich from a uniformed steward.

And what happened to that old man who had lived with them? Was he a distant relative? Or maybe he had been a boarder; it was a large house with many rooms, corridors every which way. He remembers the shoebox of ribbons and medals the old man would bring down from a closet's top shelf for bedtime stories, star-shaped and crinkly to the touch, in browns and purples and yellows. A particular story went with each decoration, stories of hardships and deprivation and courage in the face of impossible odds and of an old-fashioned honor. Some tales were of killings, both just and unjust.

"He had a huge saber in a steel scabbard. It had a brass basket guard with brass wire wound around the grip and it stood in the corner of his closet. He'd let me play with it at bedtime while he told me these tall stories about the old frontier. The sword was twice my size."

"What happened to it?" his companion asks, peering into his cup and then drinking the last of his tea. "Swords like that are very rare these days. You could probably get a lot for it." The man looks around the room for a place to put down the cup and saucer, but there are no flat surfaces near the window. Courtesy mixed with a little deference keeps the man standing, holding the empty cup and saucer.

"The old man had marvelous stories about the Indians, of how they lived and buried their dead. He had a shoebox full of items he had found in their burial mounds. Trinkets and clay figurines, pieces of fabric. Arrow points and the heads of small hatchets. He loved the Indians, even though his duty was to kill some of them."

"Will you excuse me," his colleague interrupts. "I'm taking the evening flight out. You're not leaving until tomorrow morning, are you? Until next time, then, and a pleasant journey." The colleague leaves him by the window. The clouds have pulled across the city, seemed to have cooled and become lead.

Had the old man died that summer? Perhaps that was the reason they had moved out of the house, or perhaps they had moved only to get away from the old man and his boxes of faded ribbons, to distance themselves from the clank of his saber in the corner of his closet. Perhaps he had ended his days in an old soldiers' home, talking of the prairies, the way of a horse, and about the Indians. In such a place, his medals would be ordinary, for there would be many such shoeboxes with similar contents, nor would a saber be a novelty.

In the short distance between the building's main door and the taxi stand, he is able to take several breaths of the heavy, charged atmosphere. The purified air of the hotel seems pallid and worthless in contrast, like drinking water converted from the sea, wet enough and cool enough yet strangely unsatisfying to thirst.

The address comes to his lips as if pinned to his memory, as it once had been fixed to his shirt pocket before he started off to school. But just as he repeats the address, the cab's driver turns about to look at him quizzically.

"I heard you the first time," the man says. "That's across town, and it will be dark soon."

"And?" He forces the issue, but the cabbie merely shrugs after studying him closely, turns, and puts the car in motion.

A store here, the curve of an avenue, a monument, and each landmark fits into the gaps of his remembrance. He sees the driver's annoyance reflected in the rearview mirror when he opens the window to let the hot wind caress his face. The car's air-conditioning is quickly replaced by the atmosphere outside, a mixture of fumes and odors that seem on the point of an explosive fusion.

Farther on, the streets broaden, and there are more trees; the stores are less pretentious. An old motion picture theater has become a garage, but the yarn store is still in business on the opposite corner. His mother would spend hours looking over and comparing the colored bundles of wool, the swatches of material. The cab swerves around a sharp curve in the boulevard. Here trolley wheels once grated against the polished tracks, and, coming home from downtown at night, he had pressed his face against the glass window, hands held as blinders, to see the sparks.

The tracks have been removed, but it's remarkable, he thinks, how few changes have been made in the general appearance of the area, and when the cab draws near to the old neighborhood, his pulse quickens. He has a curious apprehension that the taxi may pass a corner where someone stands who will be too awful to recognize.

At last, the cab turns onto the large avenue that traverses the street where he had lived. The large mansions that line this thoroughfare are set back deep in the gloom of their dilapidation, but they were old and rundown even when he lived here, some of them already cut up into rooming houses. Built of sandstone or brick, they are three or four stories high with grand parabolas of porches, bay windows of curved glass, and open balconies too small for anyone to stand upon and for which there were no entrances from inside anyway. Side by side, they resembled in the deepening twilight the tall, rococo sterns of ancient galleons marooned in a Sargasso Sea.

"This is where I stop. As far as I go," the driver is saying. They have pulled in to the curb. "You'll have to walk the rest of the way. Whatever your business, make it quick. That's my advice. Get out before it gets really dark."

The driver's tone is curt but not unfriendly, and he pays the man, thanks him for the advice, and gets out. The taxi makes a U-turn in the empty boulevard and drives away, and he starts to walk toward the head of the familiar street. Shadows rustle nearby, sighs, bursts of odd laughter and music. From one of the darkened houses comes the heavy verso of a saraband. One of the clouds he had watched from the comfortable penthouse of the skyscraper has just drifted over the neighborhood like a lid to seal out the last light of day and further compress the atmosphere.

Suddenly, his leather shoes are stiff and awkward against the sidewalk, so he thinks of the pleasure of this same walk when taken as a boy, barefoot in summer. This route lay between his house and the corner drugstore, a dry cleaners now he sees, and almost every summer night, the old man—the boarder—would fetch some change from his pocket and send him running for a double scoop of ice cream. On his way back, he would sometimes take a shortcut between two of the old mansions and through a vacant lot—that is still vacant. He would not go that way tonight.

He recognizes the corner of his old block. An apartment building's dim outline rises from a raised terrace that has become a knob of clay. The building was new in his day, almost fancy, and its residents envied by his parents, but it is now abandoned, windows and doors open and blank. No lights in the windows, and the remains of an automobile sprawl at the curb. The car has been salvaged on the spot and still smells of the fire that finally took it. He turns down this street.

One, two, then past a fourth, a vacant lot. A row of garages, more desolate yards, and he comes to the end of the block. He has walked past the place without recognizing it, or maybe it has been torn down to become one of the vacant lots. He retraces his steps, past the streetlamp that was the safe-home of hide-and-seek games. It is the third house from the end, and vines have grown over the front porch. But he did not recognize its smallness. He traces the roofline, the eaves and the walls and the steep stoop. The building's shape gradually develops to fill the larger image on file in his memory. Yes, this is the house.

The one light within the house burns in what he remembers as the kitchen. The people inside would be at supper now, and he recalls the old man sitting down to supper at the kitchen table, carefully peeling a boiled potato impaled on his fork. He always wore his hat at meals, a shapeless fedora. The old man's room was on the second floor, rear, and could not be seen from the street. His parents' room was in the front, and he slept in a small alcove off the bathroom, almost like a window seat. The living room was directly beneath, and on hot muggy nights they would drag mattresses downstairs and place them on the bare floor to bring them closer to the cool, musty basement below. The old man never left his bedroom.

The basement was reached by stairs from the kitchen, and the three rooms down there were given over to storage, a workshop, and the furnace, with some evidence of a summer kitchen and pantry. These basement rooms were where he played in bad weather. So many recesses and corners, so many perfect hiding places. He often forgot where he had secreted a valued toy, and then to discover it was to make it new again. Perhaps behind a molding or within a cobwebbed niche, a model car or a favorite top might still be hidden.

The steps up the porch crunch beneath his feet, the masonry rotted, but the porch seems sound. However, two wires poke through the mullion where the large brass doorbell had been installed, and he is amused by the speculation of the consequences if he were to hold the two exposed wires together. Perhaps, the house, maybe the whole neighborhood, would explode. He knocks on the screen door. The living room is very dark, but he smells cooking and something he associates with old clothes and damp upholstery. In sultry weather, a sodden aroma would waft up from the basement, welcome as if it were a sea breeze. Only a faint gleam comes from the kitchen in the rear. No sound comes through the screen door.

He knocks again. Someone must be home; the screen door seems unlatched. The evening meal occupies them. They are carefully cutting meat and methodically peeling the skin from boiled potatoes. Then without his being aware of when it happened, someone is standing on the other side of the screen door.

"I beg your pardon," he speaks into the dark where he imagines a face might be. "I'm sorry to disturb you. I'm a visitor passing through, but I used to live in this house, and since I was just passing through it seemed a chance, a good chance, to visit the old neighborhood. To see this house again. I was only a child then. It was long ago. Maybe only seven years old. Right here." No sound has come from the other side of the screen, and his eyes ache from concentrating on the darkness. He cannot see anything that even resembles the white of an eye.

"The old neighborhood hasn't changed much," he continues. "Same old streetlamp down there. The string of garages. Some of us had a clubhouse in one of them. Well, it does seem quieter. Maybe not so many children on the block now. You wouldn't believe the sound we made coming down the sidewalk on roller skates. Quite a bunch we were. Well, the house looks in good shape." He looks away from the naked wires by the door. "It's been kept up well. I guess it would be too much to ask—I don't suppose it would be possible for me to come in and look around?"

"No, I don't think so."

The answer stuns him, not its negative, which was to be expected, but the tone of the voice. It was neutral, inflectionless. Conversational. "No, I don't think so." A calm statement of opposition from the other side of the screen door, sounding bored by the necessity to say the words, as if people continually came to this door, day after night, asking for admittance, the person within patiently denying the request to look around, night after day.

"No, of course not, I quite understand," he says, catching his breath. "After all, it's your house now, and I'm only passing through, only a visitor. Actually, I lived here only a few years, not even the minimum residency of most childhoods. But tell me"—he moves closer to the screen—"if I may try your patience just a bit longer, is there still that peculiar grass in the backyard?"

"There's no grass in the backyard," the voice says tonelessly.

"Really? I would have thought it impossible to kill off. You see, an old gentleman lived here with us, or we with him, and he had been a world traveler with many stories to tell and many mementos. He had brought back from South America this peculiar grass. Two large clumps of it that made marvelous hiding places, because there was a small space within each clump where you could squat down and not be found for hours. But you had to be careful handling the stuff. If you ran your fingers the wrong way, backward along the strands, it would cut you, actually draw blood. He said in South America cattle would be driven through it to cut off ticks. On the pampas. That's what it is called—pampas grass. Very tough stuff. My parents tried to burn it out because it was always cutting me up. But it grew right back. Now it's gone. Amazing."

"Yes, gone," the voice says. A foot is shifted, a sigh—sounds of forbearance in the dark.

"This is one of the reasons I became so bold, almost was impelled to ask if I could come into the house. So many things about the old man I never knew, never understood. He had strange things in boxes. Nothing really valuable, of course"—he looks frankly into the blackness—"but trinkets, bits of stuff. Old campaign ribbons and medals. He had been a soldier too. Yellowed newspaper clippings and photographs and manuals for the maintenance of weapons that were obsolete even then. Yes, even then they were old-fashioned, out of date. But for a child my age, you can imagine—fascinating." A siren wails in a distant neighborhood.

"I just thought I could locate a few things, find stuff in places you may not know about. Old, worthless things really, but something left behind. This house has so many nooks and crannies to it. He might have left something behind. I don't suppose you found anything like that when you moved in?"

"No. Nothing."

"No, of course not. He kept all of it in a shoebox and then he had another box with things taken from . . . well, no matter. One thing he had, maybe you've come across, because it was made of steel. It was his old saber."

"What's that?"

"A saber? A saber is a long sword with a curved blade. It's one of those old-fashioned weapons that the cavalry used, soldiers on horseback in the old days. It must have been four, five feet long in its metal case."

"No sword like that here," the voice says with some anxiousness, almost hostility. "Nothing like that here. Nothing like that ever here."

"Oh but there was. I clearly remember . . ."

"I'm telling you there's no sword here."

"Well maybe not when you moved in, of course, but in the old days when I was—"

"You better go," the voice says calmly. "It's late. You shouldn't be here now. It is not good for you to be here like this."

"Yes, yes, you're right," he replies, backing away. "I'm sorry to have bothered you. I'm sorry," he adds from the top of the steps. "I'm very sorry. Truly sorry."

"Go," says the voice out of the dark.

A few scattered giggles and snorts seem to pursue him up the street to the boulevard, where they fall away, diluted by the grand illuminated vacancy of the old parkway. Here, louder cries echo within the stone verandas. The crash of a heavy door cuts short a scream.

At the corner, a modern streetlamp with a damaged filament peoples the empty intersection with sporadic shadows. It is not completely nightfall, but he sees the dancing illuminations of flames several blocks away as if a large fire were silently at work and ignored.

He turns toward the center of the city, following the scars of the old trolley tracks that have risen through the layers of macadam. To his right is a playground surrounded by a high fence of heavy mesh steel welded to substantial posts. Inside is a full-scale replica of a gingerbread house, though its peppermint candy shingles are blackened and its chimney has toppled into the hole made by the fire that gutted the playhouse. An inside job, he thinks, and laughs a little.

At last, just as the sky goes completely dark, he comes to a rise and sees the glittering prospect of the downtown skyline, dominated by the skyscraper he left earlier. Searchlights that set the building aglow enflame the clouds around the top floors, and the whole construction seems on fire. Or it appears like a huge rocket ship preparing to ignite its engines and pull itself up through the heavy clouds. He would have to hurry; he did not want to be left behind.

The Genuine Article

My sister and I would entertain the men who called upon our mother by running through the downstairs of our house in Pittsburgh, racing from the large living room, across the front hall, and into the dining room, and then back again. And then again we repeated the route to demonstrate our inner grace, our well-being, and perhaps to indicate to the gentleman caller—I think now—that our tandem versatility came as a package with our mother and if there was to be a deal, the two of us, twins but not identical, came with it. Double value.

Alix always ran ahead, her elbows stiffly held at her sides to puff out her belly, her eyes rolled back to observe the effect of her quick passage around the Queen Anne table with its dragoon of straight back chairs. I would be at her heels, sometimes having to run in place as she embellished the turn at the end of the table, and eventually devising my own innovations, a pirouette on the toes of a fairy princess was to become my signature choreography. Then we would plunge across the hallway, foolhardy girls, and into the area of the living room where the evening's audience waited patiently and with no little amazement.

Our mother would use this time provided by our divertissement to add one last note to her essential prettiness, perhaps some liner to accentuate the intensity of her blue eyes, a dab of color at the ear lobes—all enhancements we often watched clustered at her knees beneath the dressing table as we made cartoons of our faces with her lipstick in emulation. Without speaking about it, Alix and I recognized that the procedure reflected in the bedroom mirror was similar in its goal to the Olympic games we practiced on the floor below.

Our father had left us to die inconveniently in an avalanche in the French Alps, where he had been skiing during spring break from his duties at the University of Pittsburgh. Several of his students were entombed with him, and one of them, my mother was to learn later, had been his lover who had performed weekly devotions during his office hours. We were small then, just within the range of memory, and our mother was just taking her first steps up the corporate ladder of the Mellon Bank and dared not leave the city. So, our father's heedless descent beyond the piste line in Chamonix and into that frigid white permanence became a suspension that we could never completely accept. My dismissal of that poor young woman who shared his enveloping cataclysm dismays me a little now, for she had only practiced the usual sort of apprenticeship, one that would later employ me more than once, and surely a calling in Alix's world that is familiar if not worn thin. Our love for him, for with remembrance comes love, has fixed us into attitudes we cannot break through, so that young woman still caught in a schuss at twelve thousand feet is no different and possibly exemplifies the greater homage.

"I dreamed of him last night," I tell Alix. The clatter of her breakfast tray pauses. A knife poised over the jam jar? A cup hovering above its saucer? The London press has gone wild over her Blanche du Bois, and I have called to congratulate her.

"And so did I, sister. Not him so much but the scratch of his beard. I remember him hugging me that close. Scratching my cheek. I dream of his whiskers against my neck. And, I dare say, I've reproduced the sensation in my own travels."

"It was a scene," I continue quickly, determined not to let her take away my moment. "He was feeding me a cup of milk. He was cupping my face, my chin in his hand as he held the cup to my lips with the other."

I hear the clink of the coffee cup finally meeting the saucer, and the silence lengthens, as she seems to be considering the dream, but she was holding back her laughter, that boisterous guffaw that has identified her in so many crowded rooms. "My God, Cynthia, a cup of milk indeed. What a messed up pair of ladies we are. By the way, Malcolm and I are doing the splits. You'll see it in your local tabloid."

"I am sorry. He seemed right for you."

"Well, he is, but I'm not for him, I guess. My boobs are moving south."

"I can't believe that of him."

"No, I don't either. He's a good guy really. I'm just looking for a reason other than my own bitchiness. He's like Oswald Hunter. Remember Oswald? Carefully thought out Oswald."

"Yes, I remember him. A nice man." He was one of the gentlemen for whom we performed, and he hung around for a number of years. We were in high school when he finally gave up and married one of his secretaries.

"How is Mom?" Alix is asking.

"Comfortable is the operative word. Yes, clean and comfortable."

"And neat," she finishes the description and laughs deep in her throat. "Keep neat and in shape," she used to say.

"The specific rules of the aging." I join her easy laughter. "She's very happy with the place, happy with her decision to set up shop there. She plays tennis three times a week, swims, and has started a book club. The place is bright and efficient and continues to be so. She goes around with an elegant bemusement—"

"—witnessing her own meltdown," my sister finishes the thought. Then in another voice, "Yes, I can see her. Cynthia, I owe you." Suddenly it sounds as if she has dumped the breakfast tray off the bed and onto the floor. Her hotel in London is small and discreet and seems indifferent to its guests' behavior.

"No big deal. When you are here, you do your share."

"Well, it's Mom, right? She did for us. And how is Graham—well, I hope?"

"Okay and busy. We have dinner together sometimes. I'm not here a lot myself. That resort I'm doing in Belize keeps me busy."

"Oh, I could use some of that sun right now. London is special, but I'm always cold." I picture her lighting a cigarette and then looking for an ashtray, selecting a saucer from the breakfast tray. "Have you seen this movie Al Gore has done? It's pretty scary, but I wonder if someday it will get warm enough to thaw the Alps."

"That's quite an idea."

"Well, he's still there, isn't he? In there somewhere. What if the sun melted everything and he shows up?"

"I guess we would have to bury him."

"Ah, there's a loaded answer if I ever heard one. We've been chasing him downhill all our lives—it might be a little scary to catch up. Mom's been expecting him to carve a turn in the front hall."

"A ghoulish idea."

"Well, there were some heavy hitters in that bunch of cavaliers we amused."

"But not even Oswald could make the cut," I say. Her laughter is that of the girl I shared a bedroom with. "An impossible task, matching up with a ghost, though you have certainly given it the old college try." The words fall leaden from my lips; I mean to be amusing and her silence tightens my grasp on the phone. Then, she surprises me.

"Yes, you're right," she says quietly, suddenly sounding very vulnerable, which digs my regret even deeper. "I dare say, it's a quest that's put me in odd places—or should I say odd beds. But, on the other hand, have you shown Graham your complete file, sister?" She pauses and I can see her taking a deep drag on the cigarette and then grinding it out in the marmalade. "That guy on television, the so-called pundit, he was old enough to be your father. Our father."

"You win," I say and change the subject. "I'm going up to see Mom on Friday. Anything you want me to tell her? I'm taking the article in the *London Times* on you."

"Just a squeeze and a smooch. Tell her I'm sending her some fancy soaps from Whitbridge and Grey. They supply the queen's bathroom."

The drive up through Connecticut to where my mother is living goes through old territory marked by signs that point to destinations we once reached after we moved from Pittsburgh to New York. Our mother's marketing acumen had attracted a securities firm that gave her more money, more authority, and perhaps a wider field of prospects from which to fill the gap in our drawing room. So, Alix and I spent weekends in retreats set back from these discreet roads, accompanying our mother and defending her by our very presence. Our legs had become long in stiff, short skirts, and we sat knees together through a series of indifferent dinner parties, hunt breakfasts, and charity auctions as she ran her sparkling eyes over the guest list. We had become the "long-legged bait" to quote a poet, and I was too ignorant to understand the whiskied pleasantries passed to me in corners of restored farmhouses. Alix got the message quickly, and she would regale me with the details of errant fingers and unmannerly grasps of her haunch.

"Come, sir," was her favorite expression—already of the theater, "do you take me for a wanton?" She had heard the word somewhere, and we had looked it up, especially enjoying the definition "voluptuary." In any event, her corruption would be foiled when an elderly predator heard her vocabulary as that of a commanding and unexpected maturity not to be trifled with. Our laughter would exhaust us as we fell asleep in each other's arms.

Farther up is a turnoff into a bit of my own undigested history, the hard knot of its sorrow never absolved. At this crossroads where an old meeting house stands white and primly kept, I would steer my little VW bug toward the boy who made me a woman—to use the quaint terminology of the romance novel of that day. Though who made whom what in that endearing tangle of his soiled sheets is questionable, for I had chosen him as the instrument to relieve me of that virtuous burden and then, alas, he had fallen in love with me. Once, I looked over his shoulder as he negotiated my transition from girl to woman to see in a corner of his bedroom a ball and a well-worn baseball mitt, ready for play in another field and surely with the same serious enthusiasm. He continued to write me for several years and then finally quit.

So many digressions along this route, right and left, but our mother kept us moving in the direction of becoming successful women, unencumbered in our careers by a male presence that might stifle us, though she never interfered with our interest in men. In fact, I have sometimes wondered, a thought never shared with Alix, whether her insouciant display of us—little advertisements in Mary Janes—would suggest all those violations we escaped through our own dopiness had been very important to her.

The spring sunlight illuminated the faux Georgian majesty of Avon Estates, so the place looked exactly as it did in the full-color brochure Alix and I reviewed a year ago. It was beautiful and it was expensive, and it was beautiful *because* it was expensive, but our mother thought it would be right for her at this point in her life—all the comforts of home with an amiable oversight that limited unwanted socializing. If I had designed the place I would have broken up its massive structure into smaller units like English cottages, more cozy on the rocky Connecticut landscape, but our mother had slipped into that practical mode that distinguished her on Wall Street, a stern take-no-prisoners and burn-the-bridges attitude. It was simply time for her to make a change, she reasoned, and all nonessential baggage was to be left behind. The snappy, smart dispatch of her agreement was meant to remind everyone of her earlier business moves, one more proof of their rightness.

But the brilliant light also exposed the desolation of the place, extravagant desolation though it might be. Its appearance reproduced the brochures rather than the other way around. The vacant rose gardens entertained circling bees and only circling bees in their perfect glens, and several tennis courts stretched out pure and exact. And empty. About a dozen automatic sprinklers maintained a steady watery surveillance of the lush lawns. Heavy wooden benches were established here and there.

Mother was waiting for me in her apartment, wearing stylish warm-ups and sneakers and holding a tennis racket. "Right," she said promptly and made a slow forehand in my direction, but whether she acknowledged my arrival or thought she was greeting a tennis partner was difficult to tell. The pair of canaries twittered in their cage, which hung before the billowy curtains of the large bay window. It was an early-morning sound, a waking up, bird dialogue, though it was close to noon.

"Right on time. Good of you to be on the spot. I have coffee if you care for a mug." She laid the tennis racquet on the sofa's arm and stepped into the tidy kitchen corner to feel the glass pitcher of the coffeemaker. "Yes, still warm," she said almost to herself and then, "I expect you need the loo—you know the way."

I did have the need, and when I returned, she had poured me a cup with cream, just as I take it. She proffered the cup in a parody of a kind of devotion. The merry intensity of her blue eyes made a cruel commentary on the rest of her face. As she smiled, her small mouth pulled at the lines around it, and the high cheekbones, so aristocratic-looking in the picture gallery of my youth, now vainly propped up the rest of her countenance.

"Now, Cynthia, you must tell me all that has been happening with you," she said and took up the racquet again. She slid into one of the armchairs and raised one foot to rest it on her knee. It was a flexible schoolgirl pose. Her perfunctory manner had caught me up—the decorum observed for an important client or a stockholder whose vote was important. Familiar, yet at a comfortable arm's length, and I became equally formal, a daughter's dutiful review of accomplishments. As I spoke, I drew from my purse the clipping from the *Times* about Alix's London triumph and handed it to her. As she read the article, I reviewed the album of photographs on the wall by the door. Pictures of her and my father in different parts of the world, all in their youth—a handsome, complete couple smiling at the advent of their rightful destiny. She had cleared her throat once or twice in some kind of punctuation. "May I keep this?" she asked when she had finished.

"Of course, I brought it for you."

"She's almost too old for that part, isn't she? Though I guess a slut at any age has some interest." She laughed soundlessly. "She'd be good at that." I chose not to argue with her, but then she went on anyway. "I like to think I set a good model for you girls. I know it was difficult for you without a man in the house, but I had to choose between being a free agent or just someone put in a niche, in a cupboard with the best china. And both of you with me too, locked up in some presumption of what we should be."

"You did all right, Mother." This was a familiar speech.

"Yes, Alix may have been a little extreme," she continued, "barely out of high school and that Greek fisherman, I remember, with all those rings on his fingers."

"He was hardly just a fisherman," I interrupted, a little piqued. "He owned a fleet of trawlers and a couple of islands in the Mediterranean."

"Whatever," she went on, "you have to understand I respect Alix in her venery. She has always had integrity in her squalor. Is that a new purse? A Gucci?"

"Yes," I replied happy to shift subjects. "Yes, it's new, but not a Gucci.

Not a real Gucci. I got it last week down in Chinatown. There's a funny story that goes with it."

"Oh do let's have the funny story that goes with it." She sat forward in her chair, alert and lithe as if poised at the net. "Funny stories are hard to come by in this place."

"I met someone from a federal agency for lunch in Chinatown. He knows of a particular noodle place where we can go over proposals for a housing development near the Battery. It would be a nifty job for my firm. He was one of Bobby Kennedy's guys in the '60s and was very witty in his reminiscences. Lots of stories. Afterward, we walk along Canal Street, looking for a cab for me—he is planning to walk to his office farther downtown. Young Asian women keep pestering us—pestering me actually by holding out pages from magazines illustrating handbags, asking in broken English if I wanted to see such bags."

My mother gathered a towel around her neck and picked up the tennis racquet, stood, and then opened the door for me as I talked. I was to follow. "Finally Russell asks one of these girls where the bags are. She gestures for us to follow her and we do, turning up Mott Street a short distance where she opens a glass door plastered with advertisements for several teahouses, a driving school, and a travel agency. None of these are represented on the doors in the vestibule; in fact, all them are closed and unmarked, and on the landing above, the girl pauses before two other closed doors, nodding pleasantly at us."

Russell had also turned around to look down at me with a question raising his heavy eyebrows. I instantly appreciated his sensitivity. His concern. Did I wish to continue? I was a little apprehensive, but was I in danger? The idea embarrassed me a little. For a second I remembered a night of frenzied speculation Alix and I had shared after we had read a tawdry pulp novel that featured girls being carried off by Chinese white slavers to be ravished in exotic brothels. But the heroine met a man of good background who restored her to respectability, only after her corruption had been served, and so I was suddenly shamed by my hesitation. After all, I had the knowing, sturdy Russell with me, and every shift of his broad shoulders assured my safety. On the next floor above, the girl unlocked another unmarked door and led us into a simple room festooned with handbags of the most elegant and recent design.

"Prada, Gucci, Coach, Fendi—you name it," I told my mother as she led me outside. "They are all there on wooden pegs. A young Asian man is making a sales pitch to two women when we enter, and he bows slightly to acknowledge us. Our girl guide has disappeared, but in a corner another youth sits at a small table with a metal cash box, its lid thrown back. The gadgets for registering credit cards. Yes, they took plastic and probably sold it too. But the handbags feel genuine, feel like real leather. Their manufacture is photographically exact. The sales clerk holds up a large black Prada before the two women. It is covered in metal buckles and fastenings."

My mother nodded as we stepped quickly along the brick path. She set the pace, direct and resolute. Her face was thrust out expectantly for her game or perhaps the next part of my story. I could not tell if she had even been listening to me as I told her about Russell being amused by my manner, exposing me to this smarmy corner of commerce. My initiation into this illicit business raised the color in his silvery jowls, and he asked me to choose a handbag—it would be his treat. The salesman had sent the two women on their way, their purchase in a brown paper bag, a grocery bag, and then he turned to us.

"So, I pick out this Gucci," I told her. We had come to the end of the building; the tennis courts were around the corner. "But there is much bartering for this little bag. The man I am with does all the talking. I'm simply not very good at it."

"You always took the first offer," she said with a forgiving smile and looked at me sideways. Whether she relished my innocence or chided my lack of business acumen was unclear.

"Finally, the salesman blurts out, 'Fifty dollar . . . fifty dollar,' and Russell takes out his billfold and hands over the bills. The bag is slipped into another paper sack, and there you have it—this bag that would cost nine hundred dollars on Madison Avenue for fifty."

"But not the same bag, of course," my mother said wryly. "It may look the same, but it's not the same."

"I'll just walk fast past any future inspection," I said. She nodded curtly, as if I had stumbled on the correct solution. But she had also laughed. I have always wanted to amuse her, and Alix did too. I think some of my sister's egregious behavior was only to provoke a smile across those thin lips no matter how sardonic they might turn, because the expression would inject a girlish quality into her face, beyond the effect of any cosmetic, momentarily equalizing our ages, transforming her into a contemporary, a woman pal, a confidante.

For then I could have told her about the next hour of that afternoon. Russell led me up Mott Street once again and into an area where the ethnic balance shifted to Italian and then through an unmarked glass door that was also obscured by notices and advertisements. We were in the empty lobby of a small hotel. No desk clerk. Radio music played somewhere in the back of the front desk. The keyboard's mailboxes were empty, and he put some money in one of them and took a key and then jumped up the steps two at a time to the landing. He stopped and looked back at me with that same silent questioning as before. Did I want to go on? No hard feelings if not. No awkward pressure. He was a gent of the '60s and waited patiently for me on the landing to take the next step.

Curiously, the room itself resembled the other one in its simplicity, but for the addition of the bed, the sink, and the open toilet. Functional. I would not have been surprised to see more handbags hanging from the wall. The sheets looked fresh, though the enamel below one of the faucets was stained yellow. Russell set about undressing me, preparing me, removing only enough clothing for the act. He methodically fucked me at the edge of the bed, making satisfied sounds deep in his throat to accompany and approve the stages of my excitement and ultimate release. The aroma of his cologne mixed with the smell of my own rush as his large, strong hands held me in place.

Later, still within the limits of the lunch hour, we had some espresso near Bleecker Street in a small place that featured poetry readings in its back room. This day, the program was turned over to some deaf mutes who signed their poems from a brightly lit stage at the end of the room. They were youngsters who shared a scruffy sort of collegiality, and as they silently conveyed their feelings, I was reminded of Alix and me making shadow rabbits and chicken heads against our bedroom wall with an uncovered lamp. Russell folded me into a cab and turned to find another for himself. He had an appointment with the mayor downtown. The lines that had briefly intersected had now parted to put us back within other spaces, properly parallel. "I'm pretty sure I will get this job," I told my mother.

The painted lines of the tennis court gleamed in the noon hour as if the sun had ignited their pigment. We sat at the side of one court, our backs warmed a little by the sun's reflection off a practice board fixed against the wall. No one was in sight, and my mother leaned forward as if she were a line judge about to make a call.

"It's Roger," she said. "I'm trying him out and he's late. My usual partner for doubles is no longer playing, I mean not here." She smiled and answered my question by pointing toward the sky. "We lose a lot of good tennis players that way."

"You play several times a week?"

"Yes, two or three, depending on the condition of the sinews in residence." She paused to remove her jacket; her bare arms were thin but firmly muscled. Her chest and torso were trim, and I could tell she wore no brassiere. Across the way, a couple her age stepped briskly around the path near the rose garden. The woman's short arms swung vigorously like pendulums, and her companion's nose speared the air of their advance.

"It's funny," she had gone on. "I used to think I would end up murdered as part of a love triangle. A fantasy of my Presbyterian upbringing probably. But it became more and more difficult to find the other two partners for that game. Impossible in a place like this."

"Well, Mother, we'll find you another place if you are unhappy here."

"It would be no different." She waved me off and stroked my arm to quell my annoyance.

"Whatever happened to Oswald Hunter?" I asked after a bit.

The name disengaged her thought, and she made adjustments as the track in her mind changed. Her expression had become blank, and I could almost see the files being opened and sorted, old journals flipped through. Then she cleared her throat. "Yes, Oz Hunter," she said finally. "He was a sweetie. I think I saw his obit a little while ago in the *Times*. You girls liked him especially, didn't you?"

"He seemed like a good prospect."

"Good hands, as they say on the sports pages," she continued and looked carefully along the top of the net. "He particularly liked my ratatouille. But he wasn't right. Not the genuine article."

"But what would that be, Mother? Where would that be found?"

My outburst took me by surprise, but she appeared unmoved. She continued to look across the court and into the distance beyond the proper grounds. She had become inaccessible and had slipped into something more protective. It was like blaming an animal for lack of speech, and I was a little ashamed.

"In all probability," she said finally in the voice of an important portfolio manager, "your father would be dead by now anyway. I mean really dead. Yes, really dead."

After a bit, I asked, "Do you think Roger has been mislaid?"

"More likely something's distracted him, and he's forgotten. As I said, we have never played, but I have seen him in other circumstances. Not promising for doubles, but an adequate forehand."

"You could practice against the backboard as we wait," I offered and turned around to look at the wall.

"Roger has the balls," she said. Her voice carried no suggestion of a covert meaning. She continued to look down the line of the net. "Today is Thursday isn't it? Yes, Thursday. They have a special on Thursdays—a fair pot roast in red wine. With gnocchi, which I don't care for, but you might like that. Shall we do lunch?"

Clearly, play had been suspended. I adjusted the strap of her jersey that had become folded over, smoothed it over her skin, and around the bony extrusion of her shoulder bone. She leaned a little away from me and then, clearing her throat, sat back against my side, to let me complete my adjustments. Roger never showed up, and I stayed for lunch.

The Catch

The day's catch had been put down, nose to tail across the entire floor of the foyer—on newspapers, Williams was quick to note, so that he and his wife had to step carefully around and between the fish like hikers who had come to a peculiar ford of a stream but in reverse. What looked to be the glistening surfaces of rocks were the soft sides of salmon and trout.

"What on earth?" Janice Williams exclaimed.

"On earth is right," Williams replied. "How is all this to be cooked?"

From the far side of the room, in the alcove of the reception, the director of the lodge waved to them. "Come ahead. Step through, step through," the man cried gaily. "They won't bite, in fact—"

"—they've already bitten," Williams finished the joke under his breath, though his wife nudged him. The inn manager's manner had rubbed him the wrong way from the day they had arrived in Leenane. "Looking up the old connections, are you?" the man had said to them as they registered. Nothing in the name of Williams reflected an Irish background; yet, the manager's question had neatly caught the purpose of their visit to this small village at the head of Killary Bay in Galway. What's more, he was to advise his wife later, the guy wasn't even Irish but had one of those tricked-up English accents like an actor in an old movie, maybe playing the butler. This was always the case, he told her; the English had done well here.

"The gentlemen have had some little success," this butler-turned-hotel manager was saying. A peal of fellowship rose from the taproom, and glasses knocked cozily against solid wood.

"But what's to become of all this?" They were looking back now across the expanse of dead fish. Something biblical about it, Williams thought, walking across a floor of fish. "You can't possibly serve us all this for dinner."

"Oh, my no." Their host laughed lightly. "We'll send most over to the hospital and a nursing home at the Cross. Give much of it away to the natives here. Did you have a good day? Find any relatives?"

"I'm going up for a bath. Wouldn't you like to have a drink?" Janice Williams said quickly. Another gust of laughter blew in from the taproom.

"No, I think not," Williams replied and took their room key from Mr. Gibbons. Williams enjoyed leaving the expectant look on the man's face, leaving his questions unanswered and cramped in the manager's expression. He knew his wife had wanted some time to herself, to be without him for a little, but he had felt awkward all day long, out of place where he had hoped a part of himself would find a fitting, and the fraternal order of fishermen holding forth in the bar would surely define this sense of strangeness even more.

So, when they reached their room, he went to the large window set into a recess that overlooked the road and the head of the estuary. He would be out of her way. Yet, as he looked down the long stretch of water that was Killary Bay, he was able to monitor the subtle sounds of her undressing, the discreet movements from bed to closet and then back to traveling case, and the click of a metal clasp. He tried to associate each sound with some interval in her bath preparations, visualize how she might look at each interval, for unlike most men at this stage of a marriage, or so he thought, he still took some pleasure, even pride in his wife's appearance. She worked hard at it; he would give her that, even with three children and the dents of middle age, she had somehow preserved the girl-athlete quality that had appealed to him from across the net at her parents' place on Cape Cod.

"That was sort of interesting today, wasn't it?" he said. He heard her shoes being arranged on the closet floor. He pictured the sensible walking brogues lined up even-toed in much the same way they had been positioned earlier that day on the crude planks of a peasant floor.

"Yes." Her voice came back breathily from her present chore. "And I wonder why you think it strange that people see you as Irish. Every man in the place today looked like a cousin—even a brother here and there."

"Do you think so?" he asked, only to join the dialogue, because he had already thought the same. If not like him, certainly they looked like his grandfather, his mother's father. Every old man who had passed through the one room of the farmhouse had turned toward him—to understand him better—with the same large ears that had been his grandfather's, as if they were to bring him into a better focus. Was this Petey John O'Brean's grandson, to be sure? Surely he has the O'Brean manner on him.

"Ah, Dickie-boy," his grandfather would say. "The salmon come out of the waters near Leenane with the knife and fork attached to them, ready to eat. You'll never see water so clean and so pure as the streams come down with. As a boy, I would catch a trout for supper on my way home from school. Then, I'd have a swim in the bay, cold as it was—my hairs would stand out stiff. We never lacked for anything, what little the bloody English left us." The old voice, even older in his memory, spoke to Williams as his wife sat by the open hearth of the cottage in the upper part of the village. Tea and some rock-hard scones had been produced for them. A large hound, gnawing cold potatoes, lay on the apron of the fireplace that smoked with burning turf. The aroma of the peat was rather pleasant, and for about two hours, men and women passed through the open door to meet and talk to him with a stiff formality, like people in the early hours of a war. Even their clothes looked stiff, unbending, as if just lifted from boxes that kept them for such occasions. He was referred to other cousins living in Buffalo and Pittsburgh and Brooklyn, and Williams dutifully took down names and addresses in the small notebook he carried. "No finer people," the voice continued in his head, "deceived and betrayed as they were."

Despite his discomfort of being the center of some regal audience, the afternoon went pleasantly enough because of the ease with which Janice handled the gathering; she always had a way with strangers that quickly made her a part of any group. She had started to chat with the Irish countrywomen as if they had been old classmates from Sarah Lawrence. He could hear the way she answered questions about his grandfather and about Ted Kennedy—was he in good health and was he too old to make a run for the presidency like his sainted brothers? He heard her tell them about their children, trade stories with them about the prices of things and the value of a good cup of tea with real cream. In her ensemble of tweed and cashmere, a hint of gold at her ears, she looked dressed for a play by Philip Barrie rather than Synge; yet, her tasteful attire seemed to stimulate an instant intimacy, as if the casual elegance she had brought into that smoky, low-ceilinged room was something these farm women were prepared to share, had been expecting to walk through their door.

From the open doorway of the farmhouse—he couldn't remember seeing a door on hinges—he could sight the length of the bay as it came up from the North Atlantic. Steep hills came down to the shoreline on both sides to make the estuary look even more severe. The Vikings had rowed their long ships up this narrow waterway, his grandfather had told him, and weary survivors from the ill-fated Armada had swum ashore to darken local features and introduce their own spelling of names. "We never really had it to ourselves, you know," the old man would tell him, "and then the English came to stay. Not even a front door to keep out the wind. Not even a front door." Or had that ancient voice only been making the stories up, becoming a harangue that was almost comical?

From the hotel room's window, Killary Bay offered a more gentle view as the hazy light of oncoming evening athwart its headwaters fell upon the bare sides of the far shoreline. The hard definitions of the whitewashed sides of the farmhouses, like the one they had visited this afternoon, became blurred while their thatched roofs merged with the landscape, returning to the vegetation from which they had been made.

A small car had just pulled off to the waterside of the road that passed before the lodge. Three men got out and stood for a moment, looking at the water. Williams idly fancied they might be reviewing its history as he had been doing, maybe telling the same stories his grandfather had told him over and over on the back porch in Ohio that surveyed the old apple orchard. One man looked older than the other two, the youths with a dark fall of hair over their foreheads. A father and his two sons, Williams figured, pausing to admire the vista and to recount the glorious and bloody defeats of Ireland he had heard about so many times. Come to think of it, he had heard these stories at just about this time of day. Then all three men began to remove their clothes: vests, jackets, shirts, trousers, everything off in a companionable scramble beside their car—joshing and jostling like three brothers, he thought, rather than father and sons.

"I was hoping we'd hear from old Steverino," he said. His wife continued dressing. "I mean, he has our itinerary. I expected something from him in Dublin."

"You must simply get off the boy's back." She sounded distracted, as if looking for an article to complete her ensemble. "When he has something to say, he'll write. When he has something he thinks important enough to say to you. You must understand that. He doesn't want to be embarrassed by sending you just anything."

"I'd be happy with just anything."

"He doesn't think so. Nor do I as a matter of fact."

Outside the men were down to their underwear and were removing shoes and socks. Long white shorts flapped around their knees, and they looked ready for a sport no longer played. "Why would he feel embarrassed?" he said into the window. "Just to say hello—how's it going?"

"Because, dear heart," her voice rounded the tile walls of the bathroom, "he has these high standards for the transmission of information, set for him by his father."

"But I never—"

"No, I know you didn't. Not actually. You don't have to—the rules are understood. There." She sounded peevish. "Let's not go through this again. Not now. Go down and have a drink and let me have some time to become beautiful."

Outside, the three men walked abreast down the slight slope of the bank to the water's edge and, pale limbs not hesitating, plunged into the water with an ageless glee.

"Go, get out of my hair," she urged him.

His preference for being with her—even talking to her through the door of the bathroom—was another example of what she had just called getting off their backs. He never wanted to interfere with any of them, any of their endeavors, but this yen to be in their company had the same effect. The three men splashed and paddled in the water, shouting to each other and laughing.

The long hallway outside the room was heavily timbered, and the slanted floor creaked under his tread. He could imagine walking down a companionway of one of those ill-fated Spanish galleons. But then the character of the interior abruptly changed at the top of the stairs, and the décor became that of an English country manor, newels and banisters as solid and noble as the Empire. At midlanding, he was astonished to see all the fish had disappeared. Another biblical miracle, perhaps, here in western Ireland. Not even a remnant of odor remained to suggest their presentation, and when he reached the bottom step, the aromas of malt and grain wafted from the taproom, heavily sensual.

The place was not as crowded as he had feared; some of the fishermen had moved on to dine. Only a few sportsmen still held court at one end of the dark bar. The room was a polished composition of woods, glass, and metals—it must be pictured in some travel magazine—and the paneled ceiling was redolent with tobacco and whiskey smells and the dark scent like damp velvet produced by centuries of fires in the huge mantled hearth. To this mixture, the pungency of perfumes was mixed, spiced by the tinkle of jewelry and laughter from about a half dozen women who occupied a heavy table near the open French doors that faced the road. Williams paused just inside the doorway.

Behind the bar, and obviously master of the evening's revels, stood Mr. Gibbons. The manager had changed costumes and wore a mustard-colored vest, a crisp white shirt, and a tartan bow tie. Even his face looked refurbished, as if it had been thrust back into its original mold, and he raised his eyebrows and invited Williams to a place at the bar.

"Ah, now, Mr. Williams. What may I do you for?"

"I guess some whiskey, thank you."

"Something from Cork?"

"That will do."

"Or perhaps something from County Offaly. Tullamore Dew. Give the man his dew," Mr. Gibbons played out the slogan of the brand, and when he saw no recognition on Williams's face, he continued like the boy in class who had just correctly spelled the difficult word. "It's an old whiskey with the initials of its early owner—Daniel E. Williams—D-E-W, don't you see? Why, bless us—perhaps some of your family, Mr. Williams. Maybe so."

"Good enough, I'll try it." Williams said quickly to quell the lecture. Yet, he was grateful for the deft manner in which Gibbons had seated him, away from the boastful bunch at the other end. Clearly, as a professional host the man was adept at recognizing differences in his guests, not mixing them, eager to please them all. Williams felt a little chagrined by his own arrogance that had misread the man's intention.

"This is your high season." Williams sought an exchange with Mr. Gibbons when he returned with the whiskey neat and a small pitcher of water on the side. No ice.

"It is that," the manager replied. He looked carefully at his guest, trying to judge whether Williams really wanted to talk or was merely being polite. "When the salmon run, we have to quick march to be sure; some of our guests go back generations, you know. It's a place to come for the salmon."

"All from England, are they?"

"You can say that," Mr. Gibbons said and shifted his head slightly to indicate the men behind him. "Most book their rooms year in and out—year after year."

"I know," Williams replied. "The travel people said we were lucky to get a room."

"Sir Harold Fitzhugh canceled out. Some sortie with the Common Market, I'm afraid, ruined the fishing for him. He's the chief there, you know." Mr. Gibbons had confided this information amiably as he wiped a cloth over the lustrous finish of the bar top, then refolded his napkin and patted it down on one side, ready for another go, another time. "But I'm pleased we had the space for you and Mrs. Williams. Fishing of a different sort, isn't it, and just as important?"

Williams sipped his whiskey, enjoying its smooth burn down his throat and the charred wood flavor curling around his tongue. He was unable to reply. Moreover, the man's attitude had nicked him again, though he could see no sign of mockery in the host's demeanor. So, he finally said, "Yes, we had a very interesting afternoon. Strange to come on so many cousins all at once."

"They're fine people here," Mr. Gibbons assured him. "Not much in their pockets of course, and too many mouths to feed because of their way of looking at things. It's their business of course. And not to include yours now"—he leaned over the bar—"you have to watch them close, you know." He had cocked a bright eye at a busboy who had just left the room with a tray of dirty glasses.

One of the gregarious anglers called Mr. Gibbons, and the manager quickly answered the summons, leaving Williams with a hard sourness in his belly. It was probably the whiskey that he wasn't used to drinking straight and without ice, though he understood it was the right way to enjoy the local beverage. But it was Gibbons's snuggery spread over the old calumnies, the same that had fueled his grandfather's rages on that back porch in Ohio. So, his own words had come up to answer the manager, but they had been stoppered by the whiskey going down, slipping into the pit of his stomach to turn in the acid of their own anger. Ulcers started that way, he had heard.

The distance between the busboy's wrist and the sleeve of his mustard-colored jacket supplied by the hotel touched Williams, and that raw exposure of pink flesh was cruelly innocent and suspicious all at once. Something about that young Irish boy's bone and tendons called up his grandfather's neck when it stretched above the starched white collar to lend a point of exclamation to his anger. ". . . So I walked the whole distance back to the quartermaster and returned the part of the pay that wasn't mine, and I was still passed over for promotion." The laughter had been dry and knowing.

"So what?" Williams's children would shrug and look away—not all at once, but at different times, the same response. He wondered if a void within him absorbed the right words before he could pronounce them, for if he could say them his children's impatience with the repetition of the old stories of betrayals and denials might be quelled. Often, he would picture the moment: where it might happen, in a corner of their library-den or by the small pond in the back of the house, and how the young face would suddenly become serious, look deeply for the first time into something not visible to ordinary vision.

But then, one of them—or all of them—would say, "But look at you. That isn't your story. You're a success—these old stories have nothing to do with you anymore. And they would laugh at him, for they were proud of him and his success—or his wife would assure him in the same tone of appeasement she used when talking to the children.

"You must listen to your father," she would say, which sounded to him sometimes as if she were granting them a liberty *not* to listen. Lately, it occurred to him that her role as a moderator actually kept him apart from the children, like a referee stepping between fighters, rather than permitting them to settle their differences by speaking directly to each other.

Just then, laughter from the table nearby disturbed his thinking. Most of the fishermen had left the taproom to dress for dinner, but two had lagged behind to joke and flirt with the women. Their voices tagged them as English upper class, or what sounded like upper class to him, an American. Indeed, could any one of the women become caught by the lures being played around them by these passionate and tipsy anglers? Their clothes suggested an abandonment of London shops for the ateliers of Paris and Milan, and his speculation turned to other betrayals. What, after all, did these women do in a place like this while their husbands kept their footing in treacherous currents?

Wasn't there a wonderful story about this sort of thing? He tried to remember the author's name as he signaled Mr. Gibbons for a refill. It came to him as the manager brought the bottle of Tullamore Dew and poured a generous dollop. William Humphrey had written about a fishing lodge on a river in Scotland, a place where salmon spawned and where, the humorous narrative implied, the sportsmen's consorts performed their own leaps against the current while their men were away. He couldn't remember all the details, who the rogue fisherman in the tale was, but to round out his fancy, he wondered who might be baiting the hook here on the banks of Killary Bay.

"There you have it, Mr. Williams," his host said pleasantly. The man's whippet attentiveness made Williams smile. "Fine whiskey it is," Gibbons announced and returned to other duties behind the bar.

The road outside had become strangely busy. Pedestrians passed quickly before the open French doors. Their country dress of caps, thick jackets, and dark wool stockings on the women was such a startling contrast to the smartly dressed women in the taproom that Williams felt he might be watching a film, that the open doorways of the inn were actually screens upon which the old film was being projected. But this was no entertainment the lodge provided. Confusion edged Mr. Gibbon's sharp profile as he came around the bar to pass through one of the doorways and onto the lawn to look down the road in the direction the townspeople were headed. Then he joined the rush.

"Something's up," one of the women at the table said and pushed back her chair.

"A little excitement at last," another said and joined her, and then all of them were standing with a click and whisk of jewelry and silk. A few took their drinks with them out on the lawn to become onlookers.

Williams left his whiskey on the bar and followed them. The crowd had collected around the small car at the side of the road, and by the time he reached the spot, two men were taking turns trying to revive a man on the ground. He lay belly up, and his flesh was sickly pallid, perhaps never meant to be seen this way. The face had a bluish-green cast to it, as if bruised by a rough landing. Long white undershirts and shorts were wrapped wetly around his loins, and he resembled an old-time long-distance runner who had collapsed at the finish line, out of breath.

"Oh, Da, oh, Da, Da," one of the man's sons cried as the two men worked on the man on the road, and a third villager cheered them on.

"Give it to him, lads. There now, don't be shy with him. Get into it, man. Can't you do better than that?"

The drowned man was not unknown to the locals, and they spoke to him. "Come now, Pat, stop holding your breath. Give us a shout."

He was from a small place in County Mayo, just up the road. He was a farmer. He and his sons had been to market below Leenane and had decided to have a swim on their way home. It was a ritual they kept and had done for generations. Williams encountered the women from the lodge as they moved graciously through the crowd, as if distributing some sort of largesse. The ice in their drinks made no sound. "Poor man," one said to another as she adjusted an earring. Now a priest had crouched over the man.

"Ah, no . . . Da . . . no," one youth implored. His brother embraced him, they both looked down on the priest giving the last rites, looked expectantly as if this operation might succeed where the earlier effort had failed. The two men who had been doing the CPR stood within the circle of onlookers, their sleeves rolled up and chests bared like fighters who had just finished in a draw. A villager pounded one of them on the back, and the fellow looked away modestly. Suddenly, like a brightly feathered land bird lighting among gulls, Mr. Gibbons was everywhere managing and directing.

"Here now, we can put him in the boat house until his people come for him," he said. "That's the ticket, lift him right, boys." He led the way, pushing back the crowd to make a small avenue for the corpse to be carried through and across the road and into a whitewashed building, completely open in front. Inside, several fishing boats were racked upside down, and the dead man was laid onto the lapstraked hull of one of these. Meanwhile, the crowd had begun to disperse. Williams saw his fellow guests were halfway back to the lodge, stepping daintily over the unevenness of the unpaved road. Some of the women walked arm in arm, and, just as they reached the inn, his wife appeared in one of the French doors.

One of the dead man's sons had got into their car, and a couple of locals gave it a push to get it started. The young man hunched over the steering wheel, looking straight ahead, as the car jerked and bucked into life. The younger brother sat on a keg in the opening before the boathouse, his head in his hands. Someone handed him his clothes, and he looked at them as if he might not claim them or ever wear them again, then slowly he pulled on the pants. Williams realized right then that the other brother had driven off in his underwear.

"Someone drowned?" Janice Williams spoke as she approached him.

"More like a heart attack," he told her. They walked slowly back to the lodge. The light had slipped deeper into an eerie quality, like that of an eclipse, and the meager color of the landscape and the flat gray of the bay had become almost one. She reached and took his hand, and he felt strangely comforted. "It's a terribly cold body of water," he heard himself say. "I expect the shock of it might have knocked him off."

"What a tragedy," she said. "Coming in the middle of . . . ," and she fell silent. After a few more steps, she turned. "You mustn't let this upset you."

Her consolation surprised him a little, as if there was a need to console him or that she had come upon that need unexpectedly. He pulled his hand away and searched through some change in his pants pocket. "Why should I be upset? The guy knew what he was doing." The glow from the taproom spilled out through the open French doors to carpet the lawn. Some of the fishermen, a few of them in regimental pinks with ribbons on their chests, had joined their wives and were being told of the event. Before stepping through the door, Williams looked back. He could barely make out the shape of the boathouse, but a lantern had been lit and placed on the ground to mark the spot. The silhouette of the one son was barely visible, but he was there.

A second whiskey had been placed beside the one he had left on the bar, and Mr. Gibbons, accompanied by a young employee, was making the rounds of his guests, taking orders for drinks. "On the house," he invited eagerly. "On the house."

"It's like a plane having trouble," Janice Williams said. "You remember that time coming back from Paris and there was some problem with the flaps and the plane had to circle and circle until the problem was sorted out. We were all loaded by the time we got on the ground—they kept pouring free booze into us."

"I do remember," he said, and his arm went around her. The memory with its core of terror had refreshed their intimacy and affection. "Maybe we could call Steve, and maybe he would join us in Rome."

"Just like that?" She looked at him with amusement. "Leave his job and join the old folks on holiday."

"Well of course not—it's not possible." He felt himself blushing. "I just feel that more chances should be given out. Not so much time but chances. You understand?"

"I'll have a sherry, Mr. Gibbons, thank you very much," she told their host who had come to them.

The dining room on the other side of the foyer also had French windows that fronted the road, and they had been seated at a table before one of them. Several tables of sportsmen and their ladies were in the center of the room, and Mr. Gibbons moved around and through this boisterous group, pausing to lift a bottle of wine from its cooler, passing a pleasantry, or offering a discreet pat upon a uniformed shoulder. Williams admired the man's finesse, a great performance. The scene resembled something out of a Regency drama or a print by Rowlandson. All it needed were several spaniels chasing each other around the chair legs. A thick-legged waitress set down a tray near them. The busboy with the short-sleeved jacket assisted her in serving them. Thick slabs of salmon were daubed by a heavy white sauce that had some reference to dill. Boiled potatoes lolled to one side next to a pile of greenish vegetable.

"Well, the fish will be fresh," Janice Williams said as she scraped the sauce off to one side.

"And the potatoes," he said. "I remember my grandfather talking about their taste over here, and he was right. They're different, aren't they?"

"Yes," she said, taking a bite, but her voice had gone flat. She handled her knife and fork methodically and in the European fashion. Williams shifted his fork from left to right hand and lifted some potato to his mouth. Then some salmon.

It was Sir Francis Drake who brought the potato to Ireland from Peru, his grandfather had told him. "They seeded the whole country with it," the old man's voice continued. Even in this dining room with the cool wind off the bay blowing upon him, Williams could feel the summer heat of the porch steps coming through his clothes. "They were a cheap food supply that kept us going while the English took the sheep and the cattle for themselves. When the blight hit the potatoes, we had nothing. We starved. My people had the fish, at least."

"Are you enjoying the salmon?" Their turn with Mr. Gibbons had come. "Some of today's catch, and you can't beat a piece of fresh fish. I hope the unpleasantness down at the water has not spoiled your stay with us Mister and Missus." Could he not remember their name, or did he only question its authenticity? "My apologies for this awkward incident. Bad timing, for sure." He had checked their bottle and refilled their glasses as he spoke. "Can I close the widows for you?"

"No thank you," Janice Williams said. "The night air is lovely."

"It is indeed," the man replied. "As long as the gathering does not disturb you."

Only then did they notice the figures moving on the road in the darkness outside. The squarish outline of what looked like a hearse had just rolled silently by, as though pushed by the four or five people walking behind it. Then another line, all abreast, and then another. The relatives and neighbors had come to claim the farmer's body. They could hear no sounds of weeping and barely the shuffle of feet upon the gravel road, and once again Williams felt he was watching an old movie, a silent movie of an ancient tragedy. And wasn't this typical? he thought. The peasants parading their dead for the amusement of the English gentry dining on fine china. Most of the fishermen in the room bent over their plates or threw back their heads in uproarious pleasure. Outside, the quiet procession continued, and he wondered if the sounds of grief would come later, would be added to the silent parade when the stunned senses regained their articulation.

The road was empty as well as dark. The last party of mourners had moved along the curve around the bay and into the night. Williams looked into the blackness, trying to make out the figures as they became phantoms. Sea birds put out a last few cries. He could not be sure if these were actual shapes on the road or something moving only in his imagination, but in either case, their passage pulled at something within him. He stood up from the table, and he was tempted to run after them, up the road to join the group on its way to the graveyard. There, he might return all the old stories put into his head, bury them and give them back to their source. Maybe then the angry gift of them would be eased from his grasp, no longer to catch in his throat.

"What are you doing out there?" His wife's voice startled him, for he had been standing outside the French windows, holding his napkin in one hand. She looked amused but just a little worried. "Are you all right?"

"They've gone, I guess," he answered. "I'm okay." The night had become almost lush, and he laughed in embarrassment. The illusions had disappeared, finally gone as the last of the western light returned stone and reed to earth.

Self-portrait

HILARY MASTERS is the author of nine novels, two other story collections, a memoir, a collection of personal essays, and a book-length essay on a Mexican mural. He is the recipient of an American Academy of Arts and Letters Award for Literature, the Balch Prize for Fiction, and the Monroe Spears Prize (for his essays). His work has appeared in *Best American Short Stories, Best American Essays,* and *Pushcart Prize* anthologies. He is a professor of English and creative writing at Carnegie Mellon University in Pittsburgh, Pennsylvania.